W9-AJG-512

EX LIBRIS

VINTAGE CLASSICS

CATHEDRAL

Raymond Carver was born in Clatskanie, Oregon in 1938. He married early and for years writing had to come second to earning a living for his young family. Despite some early publication by small presses, it was not until the success of *Will You Please Be Quiet, Please?* (1976) that his work began to reach a larger audience. This was the year he gave up alcohol, and in 1977, after the break-up of his marriage, he met the writer Tess Gallagher with whom he spent the last eleven years of his life. During this prolific period he wrote three collections of stories, *What We Talk About When We Talk About Love*, *Cathedral* and *Elephant*. *Fires*, a collection of essays, poems and stories, appeared in 1985, followed by three further collections of poetry. He completed his last book of poems, *A New Path to the Waterfall*, shortly before his death in 1988.

ALSO BY RAYMOND CARVER

Fiction

Furious Seasons

What We Talk About When We Talk About Love

Will You Please Be Quiet, Please?

Elephant

Where I'm Calling From: The Selected Stories
(with the author's foreword)

Short Cuts
(selected and with an introduction by
Robert Altman)

Call if You Need Me: The Uncollected Fiction & Prose
(edited by William L. Stull with a foreword by
Tess Gallagher)

Beginners

Poetry

Near Klamath

Winter Insomnia

At Night the Salmon Move

Where Water Comes Together with Other Water

Ultramarine

In a Marine Light: Selected Poems

A New Path to the Waterfall
(with an introduction by Tess Gallagher)

All of Us: The Collected Poems
(edited by William L. Stull)

Essays, Poems, Stories

Fires

No Heroics, Please

RAYMOND CARVER

Cathedral

VINTAGE BOOKS
London

Published by Vintage 2009

8 10 9 7

Copyright © Tess Gallagher 1993

This book is sold subject to the condition that it shall not,
by way of trade or otherwise, be lent, resold, hired out,
or otherwise circulated without the publisher's prior
consent in any form of binding or cover other than that
in which it is published and without a similar condition,
including this condition, being imposed on the
subsequent purchaser

Some of the stories in this collection originally appeared in the
Following magazines: *Antaeus*, *The Antioch Review*, *The Atlantic*,
Esquire, *Grand Street*, TV *North American Review*, *The Paris
Review* and *Ploughshares*. 'The Bridle', 'Chef's House' and 'Where
I'm Calling From' originally appeared in the *New Yorker*.

First published in the United States in 1983 by
Alfred A. Knopf, New York

First published in Great Britain in 1984 by
Harvill

Vintage
Random House, 20 Vauxhall Bridge Road,
London SW1V 2SA

www.vintage-classics.info

Addresses for companies within The Random House Group Limited
can be found at: www.randomhouse.co.uk/offices.htm

The Random House Group Limited Reg. No. 954009

A CIP catalogue record for this book
is available from the British Library

ISBN 9780099530336

The Random House Group Limited supports The Forest Stewardship
Council® (FSC®), the leading international forest-certification
organisation. Our books carrying the FSC label are printed on
FSC®-certified paper. FSC is the only forest-certification scheme
supported by the leading environmental organisations, including
Greenpeace. Our paper procurement policy can be found at
www.randomhouse.co.uk/environment

Printed and bound by CPI Group (UK) Ltd, Croydon, CR0 4YY

For Tess Gallagher and
in memory of John Gardner

A NOTE ON THE TEXT

The text of the stories in this edition of *Cathedral* reproduces that of the first American edition (Alfred A. Knopf, 1983) and that of the first British edition (Collins Harvill, 1984). An alternate version of the story "A Small, Good Thing" appears in *What We Talk about When We Talk about Love* (1981) under the title "The Bath".

CONTENTS

Feathers

This friend of mine from work, Bud, he asked Fran and me to supper. I didn't know his wife and he didn't know Fran. That made us even. But Bud and I were friends. And I knew there was a little baby at Bud's house. That baby must have been eight months old when Bud asked us to supper. Where'd those eight months go? Hell, where's the time gone since? I remember the day Bud came to work with a box of cigars. He handed them out in the lunchroom. They were drugstore cigars. Dutch Masters. But each cigar had a red sticker on it and a wrapper that said IT'S A BOY! I didn't smoke cigars, but I took one anyway. "Take a couple," Bud said. He shook the box. "I don't like cigars either. This is her idea." He was talking about his wife. Olla.

I'd never met Bud's wife, but once I'd heard her voice over the telephone. It was a Saturday afternoon, and I didn't have anything I wanted to do. So I called Bud to see if he wanted to do anything. This woman picked up the phone and said, "Hello." I blanked and couldn't remember her name. Bud's wife. Bud had said her name to me any number of times. But it went in one ear and out the other. "Hello!" the woman said again. I could hear a TV going. Then the woman said, "Who is this?" I heard a baby start up. "Bud!" the woman called. "What?" I heard Bud say. I still couldn't remember her name. So I hung up. The next time I saw Bud at work I sure as hell didn't tell him I'd called. But I made a point of getting him to mention his wife's name. "Olla," he said. Olla, I said to myself. *Olla*.

"No big deal," Bud said. We were in the lunchroom drinking coffee. "Just the four of us. You and your missus, and me and Olla. Nothing fancy. Come around seven. She feeds the baby at six. She'll put him down after that, and then we'll eat. Our place isn't hard to find. But here's a map." He gave me a sheet of paper with all kinds of lines indicating major and minor roads, lanes and such, with arrows pointing to the four poles of the compass. A large X marked the location of his house. I said, "We're looking forward to it." But Fran wasn't too thrilled.

That evening, watching TV, I asked her if we should take anything to Bud's.

"Like what?" Fran said. "Did he say to bring something? How should I know? I don't have any idea." She shrugged and gave me this look. She'd heard me before on the subject of Bud. But she didn't know him and she wasn't interested in knowing him. "We could take a bottle of wine," she said. "But I don't care. Why don't you take some wine?" She shook her head. Her long hair swung back and forth over her shoulders. Why do we need other people? she seemed to be saying.

We have each other. "Come here," I said. She moved a little closer so I could hug her. Fran's a big tall drink of water. She has this blond hair that hangs down her back. I picked up some of her hair and sniffed it. I wound my hand in her hair. She let me hug her. I put my face right up in her hair and hugged her some more.

Sometimes when her hair gets in her way she has to pick it up and push it over her shoulder. She gets mad at it. "This hair," she says. "Nothing but trouble." Fran works in a creamery and has to wear her hair up when she goes to work. She has to wash it every night and take a brush to it when we're sitting in front of the TV. Now and then she threatens to cut it off. But I don't think she'd do that. She knows I like it too much. She knows I'm crazy about it. I tell her I fell in love with her because of her hair. I tell her I might stop loving her if she cut it. Sometimes I call her "Swede". She could pass for a Swede. Those times together in the evening she'd brush her hair and we'd wish out loud for things we didn't have. We wished for a new car, that's one of the things we wished for. And we wished we could spend a couple of weeks in Canada. But one thing we didn't wish for was kids. The reason we didn't have kids was that we didn't want kids. Maybe sometime, we said to each other. But right then, we were waiting. We thought we might keep on waiting. Some nights we went to a movie. Other nights we just stayed in and watched TV. Sometimes Fran baked things for me and we'd eat whatever it was all in a sitting.

"Maybe they don't drink wine," I said.

"Take some wine anyway," Fran said. "If they don't drink it, we'll drink it."

"White or red?" I said.

"We'll take something sweet," she said, not paying me any attention. "But I don't care if we take anything. This is your show. Let's not make a production out of it, or else I don't want to go. I can make a raspberry coffee ring. Or else some cupcakes."

"They'll have dessert," I said. "You don't invite people to supper without fixing a dessert."

"They might have rice pudding. Or Jell-O! Something we don't like," she said. "I don't know anything about the woman. How do we know what she'll have? What if she gives us Jell-O?" Fran shook her head. I shrugged. But she was right. "Those old cigars he gave you," she said. "Take them. Then you and him can go off to the parlor after supper and smoke cigars and drink port wine, or whatever those people in movies drink."

"Okay, we'll just take ourselves," I said.

Fran said, "We'll take a loaf of my bread."

Bud and Olla lived twenty miles or so from town. We'd lived in that town for three years, but, damn it, Fran and I hadn't so much as taken a spin in the country. It felt good driving those winding little roads. It was early evening, nice and warm, and we saw pastures, rail fences, milk cows moving slowly toward old barns. We saw red-winged blackbirds on the fences, and pigeons circling around haylofts. There were gardens and such, wildflowers in bloom, and little houses set back from the road. I said, "I wish we had us a place out here." It was just an idle thought, another wish that wouldn't amount to anything. Fran didn't answer. She was busy looking at Bud's map. We came to the four-way stop he'd marked. We turned right like the map said and drove exactly three-tenths miles. On the left side of the road, I saw a field of corn, a mailbox, and a long, graveled driveway. At the end of the driveway, back in some trees, stood a house with a front porch. There was a chimney on the house. But it was summer, so, of course, no smoke rose from the chimney. But I thought it was a pretty picture, and I said so to Fran.

"It's the sticks out here," she said.

I turned into the drive. Corn rose up on both sides of the drive. Corn stood higher than the car. I could hear gravel crunching under the tires. As we got up close to the house, we could see a garden with green things the size of baseballs hanging from the vines.

"What's that?" I said.

"How should I know?" she said. "Squash, maybe. I don't have a clue."

"Hey, Fran," I said. "Take it easy."

She didn't say anything. She drew in her lower lip and let it go. She turned off the radio as we got close to the house.

A baby's swing-set stood in the front yard and some toys lay on the porch. I pulled up in front and stopped the car. It was then that we heard this awful squall. There was a baby in the house, right, but this cry was too loud for a baby.

"What's that sound?" Fran said.

Then something as big as a vulture flapped heavily down from one of the trees and landed just in front of the car. It shook itself. It turned its long neck toward the car, raised its head, and regarded us.

"Goddamn it," I said. I sat there with my hands on the wheel and stared at the thing.

"Can you believe it?" Fran said. "I never saw a real one before."

We both knew it was a peacock, sure, but we didn't say the word out loud. We just watched it. The bird turned its head up in the air and made this harsh cry again. It had fluffed itself out and looked about twice the size it'd been when it landed. "Goddamn," I said again. We stayed where we were in the front seat.

The bird moved forward a little. Then it turned its head to the side and braced itself. It kept its bright, wild eye right on us. Its tail was raised, and it was like a big fan folding in and out. There was every color in the rainbow shining from that tail.

"My God," Fran said quietly. She moved her hand over to my knee.

"Goddamn," I said. There was nothing else to say.

The bird made this strange wailing sound once more.

5

"*Mayawe, may-awe!*" it went. If it'd been something I was hearing late at night and for the first time, I'd have thought it was somebody dying, or else something wild and dangerous.

The front door opened and Bud came out on the porch. He was buttoning his shirt. His hair was wet. It looked like he'd just come from the shower.

"Shut yourself up, Joey!" he said to the peacock. He clapped his hands at the bird, and the thing moved back a little. "That's enough now. That's right, shut up! You shut up, you old devil!" Bud came down the steps. He tucked in his shirt as he came over to the car. He was wearing what he always wore to work — blue jeans and a denim shirt. I had on my slacks and a short-sleeved sport shirt. My good loafers. When I saw what Bud was wearing, I didn't like it that I was dressed up.

"Glad you could make it," Bud said as he came over beside the car. "Come on inside."

"Hey, Bud," I said.

Fran and I got out of the car. The peacock stood off a little to one side, dodging its mean-looking head this way and that. We were careful to keep some distance between it and us.

"Any trouble finding the place?" Bud said to me. He hadn't looked at Fran. He was waiting to be introduced.

"Good directions," I said. "Hey, Bud, this is Fran. Fran, Bud. She's got the word on you, Bud."

He laughed and they shook hands. Fran was taller than Bud. Bud had to look up.

"He talks about you," Fran said. She took her hand back. "Bud this, Bud that. You're about the only person down there he talks about. I feel like I know you." She was keeping an eye on the peacock. It had moved over near the porch.

"This here's my friend," Bud said. "He ought to talk about

me." Bud said this and then he grinned and gave me a little punch on the arm.

Fran went on holding her loaf of bread. She didn't know what to do with it. She gave it to Bud. "We brought you something."

Bud took the loaf. He turned it over and looked at it as if it was the first loaf of bread he'd ever seen. "This is real nice of you." He brought the loaf up to his face and sniffed it.

"Fran baked that bread," I told Bud.

Bud nodded. Then he said, "Let's go inside and meet the wife and mother."

He was talking about Olla, sure. Olla was the only mother around. Bud had told me his own mother was dead and that his dad had pulled out when Bud was a kid.

The peacock scuttled ahead of us, then hopped onto the porch when Bud opened the door. It was trying to get inside the house.

"Oh," said Fran as the peacock pressed itself against her leg.

"Joey, goddamn it," Bud said. He thumped the bird on the top of its head. The peacock backed up on the porch and shook itself. The quills in its train rattled as it shook. Bud made as if to kick it, and the peacock backed up some more. Then Bud held the door for us. "She lets the goddamn thing in the house. Before long, it'll be wanting to eat at the goddamn table and sleep in the goddamn bed."

Fran stopped just inside the door. She looked back at the cornfield. "You have a nice place," she said. Bud was still holding the door. "Don't they, Jack?"

"You bet," I said. I was surprised to hear her say it.

"A place like this is not all it's cracked up to be," Bud said, still holding the door. He made a threatening move toward the peacock. "Keeps you going. Never a dull moment." Then he said, "Step on inside, folks."

7

I said, "Hey, Bud, what's that growing there?"

"Them's tomatoes," Bud said.

"Some farmer I got," Fran said, and shook her head.

Bud laughed. We went inside. This plump little woman with her hair done up in a bun was waiting for us in the living room. She had her hands rolled up in her apron. The cheeks of her face were bright red. I thought at first she might be out of breath, or else mad at something. She gave me the once-over, and then her eyes went to Fran. Not unfriendly, just looking. She stared at Fran and continued to blush.

Bud said, "Olla, this is Fran. And this is my friend Jack. You know all about Jack. Folks, this is Olla." He handed Olla the bread.

"What's this?" she said. "Oh, it's homemade bread. Well, thanks. Sit down anywhere. Make yourselves at home. Bud, why don't you ask them what they'd like to drink. I've got something on the stove." Olla said that and went back into the kitchen with the bread.

"Have a seat," Bud said. Fran and I plunked ourselves down on the sofa. I reached for my cigarettes. Bud said, "Here's an ashtray." He picked up something heavy from the top of the TV. "Use this," he said, and he put the thing down on the coffee table in front of me. It was one of those glass ashtrays made to look like a swan. I lit up and dropped the match into the opening in the swan's back. I watched a little wisp of smoke drift out of the swan.

The color TV was going, so we looked at that for a minute. On the screen, stock cars were tearing around a track. The announcer talked in a grave voice. But it was like he was holding back some excitement, too. "We're still waiting to have official confirmation," the announcer said.

"You want to watch this?" Bud said. He was still standing.

I said I didn't care. And I didn't. Fran shrugged. What difference could it make to her? she seemed to say. The day was shot anyway.

"There's only about twenty laps left," Bud said. "It's close now. There was a big pile-up earlier. Knocked out half-a-dozen cars. Some drivers got hurt. They haven't said yet how bad."

"Leave it on," I said. "Let's watch it."

"Maybe one of those damn cars will explode right in front of us," Fran said. "Or else maybe one'll run up into the grandstand and smash the guy selling the crummy hot dogs." She took a strand of hair between her fingers and kept her eyes fixed on the TV.

Bud looked at Fran to see if she was kidding "That other business, that pile-up, was something. One thing led to another. Cars, parts of cars, people all over the place. Well, what can I get you? We have ale, and there's a bottle of Old Crow."

"What are you drinking?" I said to Bud.

"Ale," Bud said. "It's good and cold."

"I'll have ale," I said.

"I'll have some of that Old Crow and a little water," Fran said. "In a tall glass, please. With some ice. Thank you, Bud."

"Can do," Bud said. He threw another look at the TV and moved off to the kitchen.

Fran nudged me and nodded in the direction of the TV. "Look up on top," she whispered. "Do you see what I see?" I looked at where she was looking. There was a slender red vase into which somebody had stuck a few garden daisies. Next to the vase, on the doily, sat an old plaster-of-Paris cast of the most crooked, jaggedy teeth in the world. There were no lips to the awful-looking thing, and no jaw either, just these old plaster teeth packed into something that resembled thick yellow gums.

Just then Olla came back with a can of mixed nuts and a bottle of root beer. She had her apron off now. She put the can of nuts onto the coffee table next to the swan. She said, "Help yourselves. Bud's getting your drinks." Olla's face came on red again as she said this. She sat down in an old cane rocking chair and set it in motion. She drank from her root beer and looked at the TV. Bud came back carrying a little wooden tray with Fran's glass of whiskey and water and my bottle of ale. He had a bottle of ale on the tray for himself.

"You want a glass?" he asked me.

I shook my head. He tapped me on the knee and turned to Fran.

She took her glass from Bud and said, "Thanks." Her eyes went to the teeth again. Bud saw where she was looking. The cars screamed around the track. I took the ale and gave my attention to the screen. The teeth were none of my business. "Them's what Olla's teeth looked like before she had her braces put on," Bud said to Fran. "I've got used to them. But I guess they look funny up there. For the life of me, I don't know why she keeps them around." He looked over at Olla. Then he looked at me and winked. He sat down in his La-Z-Boy and crossed one leg over the other. He drank from his ale and gazed at Olla.

Olla turned red once more. She was holding her bottle of root beer. She took a drink of it. Then she said, "They're to remind me how much I owe Bud."

"What was that?" Fran said. She was picking through the can of nuts, helping herself to the cashews. Fran stopped what she was doing and looked at Olla. "Sorry, but I missed that." Fran stared at the woman and waited for whatever thing it was she'd say next.

Olla's face turned red again. "I've got lots of things to be thankful for," she said. "That's one of the things I'm thankful for. I keep them around to remind me how much I owe Bud." She drank from her root beer. Then she lowered the bottle and said, "You've got pretty teeth, Fran. I noticed right away. But these teeth of mine, they came in crooked when I was a kid." With her fingernail, she tapped a couple of her front teeth. She said, "My folks couldn't afford to fix teeth. These teeth of mine came in just any which way. My first husband didn't care what I looked like. No, he didn't! He didn't care about anything except where his next drink was coming from. He had one friend only in this world, and that was his bottle." She shook her head. "Then Bud come along and got me out of that mess. After we were together, the first thing Bud said was, 'We're going to have them teeth fixed.' That mold was made right after Bud and I met, on the occasion of my second visit to the orthodontist. Right before the braces went on."

Olla's face stayed red. She looked at the picture on the screen. She drank from her root beer and didn't seem to have any more to say.

"That orthodontist must have been a whiz," Fran said. She looked back at the horror-show teeth on top of the TV.

"He was great," Olla said. She turned in her chair and said, "See?" She opened her mouth and showed us her teeth once more, not a bit shy now.

Bud had gone to the TV and picked up the teeth. He walked over to Olla and held them up against Olla's cheek. "Before and after," Bud said.

Olla reached up and took the mold from Bud. "You know something? That orthodontist wanted to keep this." She was holding it in her lap while she talked. "I said nothing doing. I pointed out to him they were my teeth. So he took pictures of the mold instead. He told me he was going to put the pictures in a magazine."

Bud said, "Imagine what kind of magazine that'd be. Not much call for that kind of publication, I don't think," he said, and we all laughed.

"After I got the braces off, I kept putting my hand up to my mouth when I laughed. Like this," she said. "Sometimes I still do it. Habit. One day Bud said, 'You can stop doing that anytime, Olla. You don't have to hide teeth as pretty as that. You have nice teeth now.'" Olla looked over at Bud. Bud winked at her. She grinned and lowered her eyes

Fran drank from her glass. I took some of my ale. I didn't know what to say to this. Neither did Fran. But I knew Fran would have plenty to say about it later.

I said, "Olla, I called here once. You answered the phone. But I hung up. I don't know why I hung up." I said that and then sipped my ale. I didn't know why I'd brought it up now.

"I don't remember," Olla said. "When was that?"

"A while back."

"I don't remember," she said and shook her head. She fingered the plaster teeth in her lap. She looked at the race and went back to rocking.

Fran turned her eyes to me. She drew her lip under. But she didn't say anything.

Bud said, "Well, what else is new?"

"Have some more nuts," Olla said. "Supper'll be ready in a little while."

There was a cry from a room in the back of the house.

"Not him," Olla said to Bud, and made a face.

"Old Junior boy," Bud said. He leaned back in his chair, and we watched the rest of the race, three or four laps, no sound.

Once or twice we heard the baby again, little fretful cries coming from the room in the back of the house.

"I don't know," Olla said. She got up from her chair. "Everything's about ready for us to sit down. I just have to take up the gravy. But I'd better look in on him first. Why don't you folks go out and sit down at the table? I'll just be a minute."

"I'd like to see the baby," Fran said.

Olla was still holding the teeth. She went over and put them back on top of the TV. "It might upset him just now," she said. "He's not used to strangers. Wait and see if I can get him back to sleep. Then you can peek in. While he's asleep." She said this and then she went down the hall to a room, where she opened a door. She eased in and shut the door behind her. The baby stopped crying.

Bud killed the picture and we went in to sit at the table. Bud and I talked about things at work. Fran listened. Now and then she even asked a question. But I could tell she was bored, and maybe feeling put out with Olla for not letting her see the baby. She looked around Olla's kitchen. She wrapped a strand of hair around her fingers and checked out Olla's things.

Olla came back into the kitchen and said, "I changed him and gave him his rubber duck. Maybe he'll let us eat now. But don't bet on it." She raised a lid and took a pan off the stove. She poured red gravy into a bowl and put the bowl on the table. She took lids off some other pots and looked to see that everything was ready. On the table were baked ham, sweet potatoes, mashed potatoes, lima beans, corn on the cob, salad greens. Fran's loaf of bread was in a prominent place next to the ham.

"I forgot the napkins," Olla said. "You all get started. Who wants what to drink? Bud drinks milk with all of his meals."

"Milk's fine," I said.

"Water for me," Fran said. "But I can get it. I don't want you waiting on me. You have enough to do." She made as if to get up from her chair.

Olla said, "Please. You're company. Sit still. Let me get it." She was blushing again.

We sat with our hands in our laps and waited. I thought about those plaster teeth. Olla came back with napkins, big glasses of milk for Bud and me, and a glass of ice water for Fran. Fran said, "Thanks."

"You're welcome," Olla said. Then she seated herself. Bud cleared his throat. He bowed his head and said a few words of grace. He talked in a voice so low I could hardly make out the words. But I got the drift of things – he was thanking the Higher Power for the food we were about to put away.

"Amen," Olla said when he'd finished.

Bud passed me the platter of ham and helped himself to some mashed potatoes. We got down to it then. We didn't say much except now and then Bud or I would say, "This is real good ham." Or, "This sweet corn is the best sweet corn I ever ate."

"This bread is what's special," Olla said.

"I'll have some more salad, please, Olla," Fran said, softening up maybe a little.

"Have more of this," Bud would say as he passed me the platter of ham, or else the bowl of red gravy.

From time to time, we heard the baby make its noise. Olla would turn her head to listen, then, satisfied it was just fussing, she would give her attention back to her food.

"The baby's out of sorts tonight," Olla said to Bud.

"I'd still like to see him," Fran said. "My sister has a little baby. But she and the baby live in Denver. When will I ever get to Denver? I have a niece I haven't even seen." Fran thought about this for a minute, and then she went back to eating.

Olla forked some ham into her mouth. "Let's hope he'll drop off to sleep," she said.

Bud said, "There's a lot more of everything. Have some more ham and sweet potatoes, everybody."

"I can't eat another bite," Fran said. She laid her fork on her plate. "It's great, but I can't eat any more."

"Save room," Bud said. "Olla's made rhubarb pie."

Fran said, "I guess I could eat a little piece of that. When everybody else is ready."

"Me, too," I said. But I said it to be polite. I'd hated rhubarb pie since I was thirteen years old and had got sick on it, eating it with strawberry ice cream.

We finished what was on our plates. Then we heard that damn peacock again. The thing was on the roof this time. We could hear it over our heads. It made a ticking sound as it walked back and forth on the shingles.

Bud shook his head. "Joey will knock it off in a minute. He'll get tired and turn in pretty soon," Bud said. "He sleeps in one of them trees."

The bird let go with its cry once more. "*May-awe!*" it went. Nobody said anything. What was there to say?

Then Olla said, "He wants in, Bud."

"Well, he can't come in," Bud said. "We got company, in case you hadn't noticed. These people don't want a goddamn old bird in the house. That dirty bird and your old pair of teeth! What're people going to think?" He shook his head. He laughed. We all laughed. Fran laughed along with the rest of us.

"He's not dirty, Bud," Olla said. "What's gotten into you? You like Joey. Since when did you start calling him dirty?"

"Since he shit on the rug that time," Bud said. "Pardon the

French," he said to Fran. "But, I'll tell you, sometimes I could wring that old bird's neck for him. He's not even worth killing, is he, Olla? Sometimes, in the middle of the night, he'll bring me up out of bed with that cry of his. He's not worth a nickel – right, Olla?"

Olla shook her head at Bud's nonsense. She moved a few lima beans around on her plate.

"How'd you get a peacock in the first place?" Fran wanted to know.

Olla looked up from her plate. She said, "I always dreamed of having me a peacock. Since I was a girl and found a picture of one in a magazine. I thought it was the most beautiful thing I ever saw. I cut the picture out and put it over my bed. I kept that picture for the longest time. Then when Bud and I got this place, I saw my chance. I said, 'Bud, I want a peacock.' Bud laughed at the idea."

"I finally asked around," Bud said. "I heard tell of an old boy who raised them over in the next county. Birds of paradise, he called them. We paid a hundred bucks for that bird of paradise," he said. He smacked his forehead. "God Almighty, I got me a woman with expensive tastes." He grinned at Olla.

"Bud," Olla said, "you know that isn't true. Besides everything else, Joey's a good watchdog," she said to Fran. "We don't need a watchdog with Joey. He can hear just about anything."

"If times get tough, as they might, I'll put Joey in a pot," Bud said. "Feathers and all."

"Bud! That's not funny," Olla said. But she laughed and we got a good look at her teeth again.

The baby started up once more. It was serious crying this time. Olla put down her napkin and got up from the table.

Bud said, "If it's not one thing, it's another. Bring him on out here, Olla."

"I'm going to," Olla said, and went to get the baby.

The peacock wailed again, and I could feel the hair on the back of my neck. I looked at Fran. She picked up her napkin and then put it down. I looked toward the kitchen window. It was dark outside. The window was raised; and there was a screen in the frame. I thought I heard the bird on the front porch.

Fran turned her eyes to look down the hall. She was watching for Olla and the baby.

After a time, Olla came back with it. I looked at the baby and drew a breath. Olla sat down at the table with the baby. She held it up under its arms so it could stand on her lap and face us. She looked at Fran and then at me. She wasn't blushing now. She waited for one of us to comment.

"Ah!" said Fran.

"What is it?" Olla said quickly.

"Nothing," Fran said. "I thought I saw something at the window. I thought I saw a bat."

"We don't have any bats around here," Olla said.

"Maybe it was a moth," Fran said. "It was something. Well," she said, "isn't that some baby."

Bud was looking at the baby. Then he looked over at Fran. He tipped his chair onto its back legs and nodded. He nodded again, and said, "That's all right, don't worry any. We know he wouldn't win no beauty contests right now. He's no Clark Gable. But give him time. With any luck, you know, he'll grow up to look like his old man."

The baby stood in Olla's lap, looking around the table at us. Olla had moved her hands down to its middle so that the baby could rock back and forth on its fat legs. Bar none, it was the ugliest baby I'd ever seen. It was so ugly I couldn't say anything. No words would come out of my mouth. I don't mean it was diseased or disfigured. Nothing like that. It was just ugly. It had a big red face, pop eyes, a broad forehead, and these big fat lips. It had no neck to speak of, and it had three or four fat chins. Its chins rolled right up under its ears, and its ears stuck out from its bald head. Fat hung over its wrists. Its arms and fingers were fat. Even calling it ugly does it credit.

The ugly baby made its noise and jumped up and down on its mother's lap. Then it stopped jumping. It leaned forward and tried to reach its fat hand into Olla's plate.

I've seen babies. When I was growing up, my two sisters had a total of six babies. I was around babies a lot when I was a kid. I've seen babies in stores and so on. But this baby beat anything. Fran stared at it, too. I guess she didn't know what to say either.

"He's a big fellow, isn't he?" I said.

Bud said, "He'll by God be turning out for football before long. He sure as hell won't go without meals around this house."

As if to make sure of this, Olla plunged her fork into some sweet potatoes and brought the fork up to the baby's mouth. "He's my baby, isn't he?" she said to the fat thing, ignoring us.

The baby leaned forward and opened up for the sweet potatoes. It reached for Olla's fork as she guided the sweet potatoes into its mouth, then clamped down. The baby chewed the stuff and rocked some more on Olla's lap. It was so popeyed, it was like it was plugged into something.

Fran said, "He's some baby, Olla."

The baby's face screwed up. It began to fuss all over again.

"Let Joey in," Olla said to Bud.

Bud let the legs of his chair come down on the floor. "I think we should at least ask these people if they mind," Bud said.

Olla looked at Fran and then she looked at me. Her face had gone red again. The baby kept prancing in her lap, squirming to get down.

"We're friends here," I said. "Do whatever you want."

Bud said, "Maybe they don't want a big old bird like Joey in the house. Did you ever think of that, Olla?"

"Do you folks mind?" Olla said to us. 'If Joey comes inside? Things got headed in the wrong direction with that bird tonight. The baby, too, I think. He's used to having Joey come in and fool around with him a little before his bedtime. Neither of them can settle down tonight."

"Don't ask us," Fran said. "I don't mind if he comes in. I've never been up close to one before. But I don't mind." She looked at me. I suppose I could tell she wanted me to say something.

"Hell, no," I said. "Let him in." I picked up my glass and finished the milk.

Bud got up from his chair. He went to the front door and opened it. He flicked on the yard lights.

"What's your baby's name?" Fran wanted to know.

'Harold,' Olla said. She gave Harold some more sweet potatoes from her plate. "He's real smart. Sharp as a tack. Always knows what you're saying to him. Don't you, Harold? You wait until you get your own baby, Fran. You'll see."

Fran just looked at her. I heard the front door open and then close.

"He's smart, all right," Bud said as he came back into the kitchen. "He takes after Olla's dad. Now there was one smart old boy for you."

* * *

I looked around behind Bud and could see that peacock hanging back in the living room, turning its head this way and that, like you'd turn a hand mirror. It shook itself, and the sound was like a deck of cards being shuffled in the other room.

It moved forward a step. Then another step.

"Can I hold the baby?" Fran said. She said it like it would be a favor if Olla would let her.

Olla handed the baby across the table to her.

Fran tried to get the baby settled in her lap. But the baby began to squirm and make its noises.

"Harold," Fran said.

Olla watched Fran with the baby. She said, "When Harold's grandpa was sixteen years old, he set out to read the encyclopedia from A to Z. He did it, too. He finished when he was twenty. Just before he met my mama."

"Where's he now?" I asked. "What's he do?" I wanted to know what had become of a man who'd set himself a goal like that.

"He's dead," Olla said. She was watching Fran, who by now had the baby down on its back and across her knees. Fran chucked the baby under one of its chins. She started to talk baby talk to it.

"He worked in the woods," Bud said. "Loggers dropped a tree on him."

"Mama got some insurance money," Olla said. "But she spent that. Bud sends her something every month."

"Not much," Bud said. "Don't have much ourselves. But she's Olla's mother."

By this time, the peacock had gathered its courage and was beginning to move slowly, with little swaying and jerking motions, into the kitchen. Its head was erect but at an angle, its red eyes fixed on us. Its crest, a little sprig of feathers, stood a few inches over its head. Plumes rose from its tail. The bird stopped a few feet away from the table and looked us over.

"They don't call them birds of paradise for nothing," Bud said.

Fran didn't look up. She was giving all her attention to the baby. She'd begun to patty-cake with it, which pleased the baby somewhat. I mean, at least the thing had stopped fussing. She brought it up to her neck and whispered something into its ear.

"Now," she said, "don't tell anyone what I said."

The baby stared at her with its pop eyes. Then it reached and got itself a baby handful of Fran's blond hair. The peacock stepped closer to the table. None of us said anything. We just sat still. Baby Harold saw the bird. It let go of Fran's hair and stood up on her lap. It pointed its fat fingers at the bird. It jumped up and down and made noises.

The peacock walked quickly around the table and went for the baby. It ran its long neck across the baby's legs. It pushed its beak in under the baby's pyjama top and shook its stiff head back and forth. The baby laughed and kicked its feet. Scooting onto its back, the baby worked its way over Fran's knees and down onto the floor. The peacock kept pushing against the baby, as if it was a game they were playing. Fran held the baby against her legs while the baby strained forward.

"I just don't believe this," she said.

"That peacock is crazy, that's what," Bud said. "Damn bird doesn't know it's a bird, that's its major trouble."

Olla grinned and showed her teeth again. She looked over at Bud. Bud pushed his chair away from the table and nodded.

It *was* an ugly baby. But, for all I know, I guess it didn't matter that much to Bud and Olla. Or if it did, maybe they simply thought, So okay if it's ugly. It's our baby. And this is just a stage. Pretty soon there'll be another stage. There is this stage and then there is the next stage. Things will be okay in the long run, once all the stages have been gone through. They might have thought something like that.

Bud picked up the baby and swung him over his head until Harold shrieked. The peacock ruffled its feathers and watched.

Fran shook her head again. She smoothed out her dress where the baby had been. Olla picked up her fork and was working at some lima beans on her plate.

Bud shifted the baby onto his hip and said, "There's pie and coffee yet."

That evening at Bud and Olla's was special. I knew it was special. That evening I felt good about almost everything in my life. I couldn't wait to be alone with Fran to talk to her about what I was feeling. I made a wish that evening. Sitting there at the table, I closed my eyes for a minute and thought hard. What I wished for was that I'd never forget or otherwise let go of that evening. That's one wish of mine that came true. And it was bad luck for me that it did. But, of course, I couldn't know that then.

"What are you thinking about, Jack?" Bud said to me.

"I'm just thinking," I said. I grinned at him. .

"A penny," Olla said.

I just grinned some more and shook my head.

After we got home from Bud and Olla's that night, and we were under the covers, Fran said, "Honey, fill me up with your seed!" When she said that, I heard her all the way down to my toes, and I hollered and let go.

Later, after things had changed for us, and the kid had come along, all of that, Fran would look back on that evening at Bud's place as the beginning of the change. But she's wrong. The change came later – and when it came, it was like something that happened to other people, not something that could have happened to us.

"Goddamn those people and their ugly baby," Fran will say, for no apparent reason, while we're watching TV late at night. "And that smelly bird," she'll say. "Christ, who needs it!" Fran will say. She says this kind of stuff a lot, even though she hasn't seen Bud and Olla since that one time.

Fran doesn't work at the creamery anymore, and she cut her hair a long time ago. She's gotten fat on me, too. We don't talk about it. What's to say?

I still see Bud at the plant. We work together and we open our lunch pails together. If I ask, he tells me about Olla and Harold. Joey's out of the picture. He flew into his tree one night and that was it for him. He didn't come down. Old age, maybe, Bud says. Then the owls took over. Bud shrugs. He eats his sandwich and says Harold's going to be a line-backer someday. "You ought to see that kid," Bud says. I nod. We're still friends. That hasn't changed any. But I've gotten careful with what I say to him. And I know he feels that and wishes it could be different. I wish it could be, too.

Once in a blue moon, he asks about my family. When he does, I tell him everybody's fine. "Everybody's fine," I say. I close the lunch pail and take out my cigarettes. Bud nods and sips his coffee. The truth is, my kid has a conniving streak in him. But I don't talk about it. Not even with his mother. Especially her. She and I talk less and less as it is. Mostly it's just the TV. But I remember that night. I recall the way the peacock picked up its gray feet and inched around the table. And then my friend and his wife saying goodnight to us on the porch. Olla giving Fran some peacock feathers to take home. I remember all of us shaking hands, hugging each other, saying things. In the car, Fran sat close to me as we drove away. She kept her hand on my leg. We drove home like that from my friend's house.

Chef's House

That summer Wes rented a furnished house north of Eureka from a recovered alcoholic named Chef. Then he called to ask me to forget what I had going and to move up there and live with him. He said he was on the wagon. I knew about that wagon. But he wouldn't take no for an answer. He called again and said, Edna, you can see the ocean from the front window. You can smell salt in the air. I listened to him talk. He didn't slur his words. I said, I'll think about it. And I did. A week later he called again and said, Are you coming? I said I was still thinking. He said, We'll start over. I said, If I come up there, I want you to do something for me. Name it, Wes said. I said, I want you to try and be the Wes I used to know. The old Wes. The Wes I married. Wes began to cry, but I took it as a sign of his good intentions. So I said, All right, I'll come up.

Wes had quit his girlfriend, or she'd quit him – I didn't know, didn't care. When I made up my mind to go with Wes, I had to say goodbye to my friend. My friend said, You're making a mistake. He said, Don't do this to me. What about us? he said. I said, I have to do it for Wes's sake. He's trying to stay sober. You remember what that's like. I remember, my friend said, but I don't want you to go. I said, I'll go for the summer. Then I'll see. I'll come back, I said. He said, What about me? What about my sake? Don't come back, he said.

* * *

We drank coffee, pop, and all kinds of fruit juice that summer. The whole summer, that's what we had to drink. I found myself wishing the summer wouldn't end. I knew better, but after a month of being with Wes in Chef's house, I put my wedding ring back on. I hadn't worn the ring in two years. Not since the night Wes was drunk and threw his ring into a peach orchard.

Wes had a little money, so I didn't have to work. And it turned out Chef was letting us have the house for almost nothing. We didn't have a telephone. We paid the gas and light and shopped for specials at the Safeway. One Sunday afternoon Wes went out to get a sprinkler and came back with something for me. He came back with a nice bunch of daisies and a straw hat. Tuesday evenings we'd go to a movie. Other nights Wes would go to what he called his Don't Drink meetings. Chef would pick him up in his car at the door and drive him home again afterward. Some days Wes and I would go fishing for trout in one of the freshwater lagoons nearby. We'd fish off the bank and take all day to catch a few little ones. They'll do fine, I'd say, and that night I'd fry them for supper.

Sometimes I'd take off my hat and fall asleep on a blanket next to my fishing pole. The last thing I'd remember would be clouds passing overhead toward the central valley. At night, Wes would take me in his arms and ask me if I was still his girl.

Our kids kept their distance. Cheryl lived with some people on a farm in Oregon. She looked after a herd of goats and sold the milk. She kept bees and put up jars of honey. She had her own life, and I didn't blame her. She didn't care one way or the other about what her dad and I did so long as we didn't get her into it. Bobby was in Washington working in the hay. After the haying season, he planned to work in the apples. He had a girl and was saving his money. I wrote letters and signed them, "Love always."

One afternoon Wes was in the yard pulling weeds when Chef drove up in front of the house. I was working at the sink. I looked and saw Chef's big car pull in. I could see his car, the access road and the freeway, and, behind the freeway, the dunes and the ocean. Clouds hung over the water. Chef got out of his car and hitched his pants. I knew there was something. Wes stopped what he was doing and stood up. He was wearing his gloves and a canvas hat. He took off the hat and wiped his face with the back of his hand. Chef walked over and put his arm around Wes's shoulders. Wes took off one of his gloves. I went to the door. I heard Chef say to Wes God knows he was sorry but he was going to have to ask us to leave at the end of the month. Wes pulled off his other glove. Why's that, Chef? Chef said his daughter, Linda, the woman Wes used to call fat Linda from the time of his drinking days, needed a place to live and this place was it. Chef told Wes that Linda's husband had taken his fishing boat out a few weeks back and nobody had heard from him since. She's my own blood, Chef said to Wes. She's lost her husband. She's lost her baby's father. I can help. I'm glad I'm in a position to help, Chef said. I'm sorry, Wes, but you'll have to look for another house. Then Chef hugged Wes again, hitched his pants, and got in his big car and drove away.

Wes came inside the house. He dropped his hat and gloves on the carpet and sat down in the big chair. Chef's chair, it occurred to me. Chef's carpet, even. Wes looked pale. I poured two cups of coffee and gave one to him.

It's all right, I said. Wes, don't worry about it, I said. I sat down on Chef's sofa with my coffee.

Fat Linda's going to live here now instead of us, Wes said. He held his cup, but he didn't drink from it.

Wes, don't get stirred up, I said.

Her man will turn up in Ketchikan, Wes said. Fat Linda's husband has simply pulled out on them. And who could blame him? Wes said. Wes said if it came to that, he'd go down with his ship, too, rather than live the rest of his days with Fat Linda and her kid. Then Wes put his cup down next to his gloves. This has been a happy house up to now, he said.

We'll get another house, I said.

Not like this one, Wes said. It wouldn't be the same, anyway. This house has been a good house for us. This house has good memories to it. Now Fat Linda and her kid will be in here, Wes said. He picked up his cup and tasted from it.

It's Chef's house, I said. He has to do what he has to do.

I know that, Wes said. But I don't have to like it.

Wes had this look about him. I knew that look. He kept touching his lips with his tongue. He kept thumbing his shirt under his waistband. He got up from the chair and went to the window. He stood looking out at the ocean and at the clouds, which were building up. He patted his chin with his fingers like he was thinking about something. And he was thinking.

Go easy, Wes, I said.

She wants me to go easy, Wes said. He kept standing there.

But in a minute he came over and sat next to me on the sofa. He crossed one leg over the other and began fooling with the buttons on his shirt. I took his hand. I started to talk. I talked about the summer. But I caught myself talking like it was something that had happened in the past. Maybe years back. At any rate, like something that was over. Then I started talking about the kids. Wes said he wished he could do it over again and do it right this time.

They love you, I said.

No, they don't, he said.

I said, Someday, they'll understand things.

Maybe, Wes said. But it won't matter then.

You don't know, I said.

I know a few things, Wes said, and looked at me. I know I'm glad you came up here. I won't forget you did it, Wes said.

I'm glad, too, I said. I'm glad you found this house, I said.

Wes snorted. Then he laughed. We both laughed. That Chef, Wes said, and shook his head. He threw us a knuckleball, that son of a bitch. But I'm glad you wore your ring. I'm glad we had us this time together, Wes said.

Then I said something. I said, Suppose, just suppose, nothing had ever happened. Suppose this was for the first time. Just suppose. It doesn't hurt to suppose. Say none of the other had ever happened. You know what I mean? Then what? I said.

Wes fixed his eyes on me. He said, Then I suppose we'd have to be somebody else if that was the case. Somebody we're not. I don't have that kind of supposing left in me. We were born who we are. Don't you see what I'm saying?

I said I hadn't thrown away a good thing and come six hundred miles to hear him talk like this.

He said, I'm sorry, but I can't talk like somebody I'm not. I'm not somebody else. If I was somebody else, I sure as hell wouldn't be here. If I was somebody else, I wouldn't be me. But I'm who I am. Don't you see?

Wes, it's all right, I said. I brought his hand to my cheek. Then, I don't know, I remembered how he was when he was nineteen, the way he looked running across this field to where his dad sat on a tractor, hand over his eyes, watching Wes run toward him. We'd just driven up from California.

I got out with Cheryl and Bobby and said, There's Grandpa. But they were just babies.

Wes sat next to me patting his chin, like he was trying to figure out the next thing. Wes's dad was gone and our kids were grown up. I looked at Wes and then I looked around Chef's living room at Chef's things, and I thought, We have to do something now and do it quick.

Hon, I said. Wes, listen to me.

What do you want? he said. But that's all he said. He seemed to have made up his mind. But, having made up his mind, he was in no hurry. He leaned back on the sofa, folded his hands in his lap, and closed his eyes. He didn't say anything else. He didn't have to.

I said his name to myself. It was an easy name to say, and I'd been used to saying it for a long time. Then I said it once more. This time I said it out loud. Wes, I said.

He opened his eyes. But he didn't look at me. He just sat where he was and looked toward the window. Fat Linda, he said. But I knew it wasn't her. She was nothing. Just a name. Wes got up and pulled the drapes and the ocean was gone just like that. I went in to start supper. We still had some fish in the icebox. There wasn't much else. We'll clean it up tonight, I thought, and that will be the end of it.

Preservation

Sandy's husband had been on the sofa ever since he'd been terminated three months ago. That day, three months ago, he'd come home looking pale and scared and with all of his work things in a box. "Happy Valentine's Day," he said to Sandy and put a heart-shaped box of candy and a bottle of Jim Beam on the kitchen table. He took off his cap and laid that on the table, too. "I got canned today. Hey, what do you think's going to happen to us now?"

Sandy and her husband sat at the table and drank whiskey and ate the chocolates. They talked about what he might be able to do instead of putting roofs on new houses. But they couldn't think of anything. "Something will turn up," Sandy said. She wanted to be encouraging. But she was scared, too. Finally, he said he'd sleep on it. And he did. He made his bed on the sofa that night, and that's where he'd slept every night since it had happened.

The day after his termination there were unemployment benefits to see about. He went downtown to the state office to fill out papers and look for another job. But there were no jobs in his line of work, or in any other line of work. His face began to sweat as he tried to describe to Sandy the milling crowd of men and women down there. That evening he got back on the sofa. He began spending all of his time there, as if, she thought, it was the thing he was supposed to do now that he no longer had any work. Once in a while he had to go talk to somebody about a job possibility, and every two weeks he had to go sign something to collect his unemployment compensation. But the rest of the time he stayed on the sofa. It's like he *lives* there, Sandy thought. He *lives* in the living room. Now and then he looked through magazines she brought home from the grocery store; and every so often she came in to find him looking at this big book she'd got as a bonus for joining a book club – something called *Mysteries of the Past*. He held the book in front of him with both hands, his head inclined over the pages, as if he were being drawn in by what he was reading. But after a while she noticed that he didn't seem to be making any progress in it; he still seemed to be at about the same place – somewhere around chapter two, she guessed. Sandy picked it up once and opened it to his place. There she read about a man who had been discovered after spending two thousand years in a peat bog in the Netherlands. A photograph appeared on one page. The man's brow was furrowed, but there was a serene expression to his face. He wore a leather cap and lay on his side. The man's hands and feet had shriveled, but otherwise he didn't look so awful. She read in the book a little further, then put it back where she'd gotten it. Her husband kept it within easy reach on the coffee table that stood in front of the sofa. That goddamn sofa! As far as she was concerned, she didn't even want to sit on it again. She couldn't imagine them ever having lain down there in the past to make love.

The newspaper came to the house every day. He read it from the first page to the last. She saw him read everything, right down to the obituary section, and the part showing the temperatures of the major cities, as well as the Business News section which told about mergers and interest rates. Mornings, he got up before she did and used the bathroom.

Then he turned the TV on and made coffee. She thought he seemed upbeat and cheerful at that hour of the day. But by the time she left for work, he'd made his place on the sofa and the TV was going. Most often it would still be going when she came in again that afternoon. He'd be sitting up on the sofa, or else lying down on it, dressed in what he used to wear to work – jeans and a flannel shirt. But sometimes the TV would be off and he'd be sitting there holding his book.

"How's it going?" he'd say when she looked in on him.

"Okay," she'd say. "How's it with you?"

"Okay."

He always had a pot of coffee warming on the stove for her. In the living room, she'd sit in the big chair and he'd sit on the sofa while they talked about her day. They'd hold their cups and drink their coffee as if they were normal people, Sandy thought.

Sandy still loved him, even though she knew things were getting weird. She was thankful to have her job, but she didn't know what was going to happen to them or to anybody else in the world. She had a girlfriend at work she confided in one time about her husband about his being on the sofa all the time. For some reason, her friend didn't seem to think it was anything very strange, which both surprised and depressed Sandy. Her friend told her about her uncle in Tennessee – when her uncle had turned forty, he got into his bed and wouldn't get up anymore. And he cried a lot – he cried at least once every day. She told Sandy she guessed her uncle was afraid of getting old. She guessed maybe he was afraid of a heart attack or something. But the man was sixty-three now and still breathing, she said. When Sandy heard this, she was stunned. If this woman was telling the truth, she thought, the man has been in bed for twenty-three years. Sandy's husband was only thirty-one. Thirty-one and twenty-three is fifty-four. That'd put her in her fifties then, too. My God, a person couldn't live the whole rest of his life in bed, or else on the sofa. If her husband had been wounded or was ill, or had been hurt in a car accident, that'd be different. She could understand that. If something like that was the case, she knew she could bear it. Then if he had to live on the sofa, and she had to bring him his food out there, maybe carry the spoon up to his – there was even something like romance in that kind of thing. But for her husband, a young and otherwise healthy man, to take to the sofa in this way and not want to get up except to go to the bathroom or to turn the TV on in the morning or off at night, this was different. It made her ashamed; and except for that one tirade she didn't talk about it to anybody. She didn't say any more about it to her friend, whose uncle had gotten into bed twenty-three years ago and was still there, as far as Sandy knew.

Late one afternoon she came home from work, parked the car, and went inside the house. She could hear the TV going in the living room as she let herself in the door to the kitchen. The coffee pot was on the stove, and the burner was on low. From where she stood in the kitchen, holding her purse, she could look into the living room and see the back of the sofa and the TV screen. Figures moved across the screen. Her husband's bare feet stuck out from one end of the sofa. At the other end, on a pillow which lay across the arm of the sofa, she could see the crown of his head. He didn't stir. He may or may not have been asleep, and he may or may not have heard her come in. But she decided it didn't make any difference one way or the other. She put her purse on the table and went over to the fridge to get herself some yogurt. But when she opened the door, warm, boxed-in air came out at her. She couldn't believe the mess inside. The ice cream from the freezer had melted and run down into the leftover fish sticks and cole slaw. Ice cream had gotten into the bowl of Spanish rice and pooled on the bottom of the fridge. Ice cream was everywhere. She opened the door to the freezer compartment. An awful smell puffed out at her that made her want to gag. Ice cream covered the bottom of the compartment and puddled around a three-pound package of hamburger. She pressed her finger into the cellophane wrapper covering the meat, and her finger sank into the package. The pork chops had thawed, too. Everything had thawed, including some more fish sticks, a package of Steak-ums, and two Chef Sammy Chinese food dinners. The hot dogs and homemade spaghetti sauce had thawed. She closed the door to the freezer and reached into the fridge for her carton of yogurt. She raised the lid on the yogurt and sniffed. That's when she yelled at her husband.

"What is it?" he said, sitting up and looking over the back of the sofa. "Hey, what's wrong?" He pushed his hand through his hair a couple of times. She couldn't tell if he'd been asleep all this time or what.

"This goddamn fridge has gone out," Sandy said. "That's what."

Her husband got up off the sofa and lowered the volume on the TV. Then he turned it off and came out to the kitchen. "Let me see this," he said. "Hey, I don't believe this."

"See for yourself," she said. "Everything's going to spoil."

Her husband looked inside the fridge, and his face assumed a very grave expression. Then he poked around in the freezer and saw what things were like in there.

"Tell me what next," he said.

A bunch of things suddenly flew into her head, but she didn't say anything.

"Goddamn it," he said, "when it rains, it pours. Hey, this fridge can't be more than ten years old. It was nearly new when we bought it. Listen, my folks had a fridge that lasted them twenty-five years. They gave it to my brother when he got married. It was working fine. Hey, what's going on?" He moved over so that he could see into the narrow space between the fridge and the wall. "I don't get it," he said and shook his head. "It's plugged in." Then he took hold of the fridge and rocked it back and forth. He put his shoulder against it and pushed and jerked the appliance a few inches out into the kitchen. Something inside the fridge fell off a shelf and broke. "Hell's bells," he said.

Sandy realized she was still holding the yogurt. She went over to the garbage can, raised the lid, and dropped the carton inside. "I have to cook everything tonight," she said. She saw herself at the stove frying meat, fixing things in pans on the stove and in the oven. "We need a new fridge," she said.

He didn't say anything. He looked into the freezer compartment once more and turned his head back and forth.

She moved in front of him and started taking things off the shelves and putting stuff on the table. He helped. He took the meat out of the freezer and put the packages on the table. Then he took the other things out of the freezer and put them in a different place on the table. He took everything out and then found the paper towels and the dishcloth and started wiping up inside.

"We lost our Freon," he said and stopped wiping. "That's what happened. I can smell it. The Freon leaked out. Something happened and the Freon went. Hey, I saw this happen to somebody else's box once." He was calm now.

He started wiping again. "It's the Freon," he said.

She stopped what she was doing and looked at him. "We need another fridge," she said.

"You said that. Hey, where are we going to get one? They don't grow on trees."

"We have to have one," she said. "Don't we need a fridge? Maybe we don't. Maybe we can keep our perishables on the window sill like those people in tenements do. Or else we could get one of those little Styrofoam coolers and buy some ice every day." She put a head of lettuce and some tomatoes on the table next to the packages of meat. Then she sat down on one of the dinette chairs and brought her hands up to her face.

"We'll get us another fridge," her husband said. "Hell, yes. We need one, don't we? We can't get along without one. The question is, where do we get one and how much can we pay for it? There must be zillions of used ones in the classifieds. Just hold on and we'll see what's in the paper. Hey, I'm an expert on the classifieds," he said.

She brought her hands down from her face and looked at him.

"Sandy, we'll find us a good used box out of the paper," he went on. "Most of your fridges are built to last a lifetime. This one of ours, Jesus, I don't know what happened to it. It's only the second one in my life I ever heard about going on the fritz like this." He switched his gaze to the fridge again. "Goddamn lousy luck," he said.

"Bring the paper out here," she said. "Let's see what there is."

"Don't worry," he said. He went out to the coffee table, sorted through the stack of newspapers, and came back to the kitchen with the classified section. She pushed the food to one side so that he could spread the pages out. He took one of the chairs.

She glanced down at the paper, then at the food that had thawed. "I've got to fry pork chops tonight," she said. "And I have to cook up that hamburger. And those sandwich steaks and the fish sticks. Don't forget the TV dinners, either."

"That goddamned Freon," he said. "You can smell it."

They began to go through the classifieds. He ran his finger down one column and then another. He passed quickly over the JOBS AVAILABLE section. She saw checks beside a couple of things, but she didn't look to see what he'd marked. It didn't matter. There was a column headlined OUTDOOR CAMPING SUPPLIES. Then they found it APPLIANCES NEW AND USED.

"Here," she said, and put her finger down on the paper.

He moved her finger. "Let me see," he said.

She put her finger back where it'd been. "'Refrigerators, Ranges, Washers, Dryers, etc.,'" she said, reading from the ad boxed in the column. "'Auction Barn.' What's that? Auction Barn." She went on reading. "'New and used appliances and more every Thursday night. Auction at seven o'clock.' That's today. Today's Thursday," she said. "This auction's tonight. And this place is not very far away. It's down on Pine Street. I must have driven by there a hundred times. You, too. You know where it is. It's down there close to that Baskin-Robbins."

Her husband didn't say anything. He stared at the ad. He brought his hand up and pulled at his lower lip with two of his fingers. "Auction Barn," he said.

She fixed her eyes on him. "Let's go to it. What do you say? It'll do you good to get out, and we'll see if we can't find us a fridge. Two birds with one stone," she said.

"I've never been to an auction in my life," he said. "I don't believe I want to go to one now."

"Come on," Sandy said. "What's the matter with you?

They're fun. I haven't been to one in years, not since I was a kid. I used to go to them with my dad." She suddenly wanted to go to this auction very much.

"Your dad," he said.

"Yeah, my dad." She looked at her husband, waiting for him to say something else. The least thing. But he didn't.

"Auctions are fun," she said.

"They probably are, but I don't want to go."

"I need a bed lamp, too," she went on. "They'll have bed lamps."

"Hey, we need lots of things. But I don't have a job, remember?"

"I'm going to this auction," she said. "Whether you go or not. You might as well come along. But I don't care. If you want the truth, it's immaterial to me. But I'm going."

"I'll go with you. Who said I wouldn't go?" He looked at her and then looked away. He picked up the paper and read the ad again. "I don't know the first thing about auctions. But, sure, I'll try anything once. Whoever said anything about us buying an icebox at an auction?"

"Nobody," she said. "But we'll do it anyway."

"Okay," he said.

"Good," she said. "But only if you really want to."

He nodded.

She said, "I guess I'd better start cooking. I'll cook the goddamn pork chops now, and we'll eat. The rest of this stuff can wait. I'll cook everything else later. After we go to this auction. But we have to get moving. The paper said seven o'clock."

"Seven o'clock," he said. He got up from the table and made his way into the living room, where he looked out the bay window for a minute. A car passed on the street outside. He brought his fingers up to his lip. She watched him sit down on the sofa and take up his book. He opened it to his place. But in a minute he put it down and lay back on the sofa. She saw his head come down on the pillow that lay across the arm of the sofa. He adjusted the pillow under his head and put his hands behind his neck. Then he lay still. Pretty soon she saw his arms move down to his sides.

She folded the paper. She got up from the chair and went quietly out to the living room, where she looked over the back of the sofa. His eyes were shut. His chest seemed to barely rise and then fall. She went back to the kitchen and put a frying pan on the burner. She turned the burner on and poured oil into the pan. She started frying pork chops. She'd gone to auctions with her dad. Most of those auctions had to do with farm animals. She seemed to remember her dad was always trying to sell a calf, or else buy one. Sometimes there'd be farm equipment and household items at the auctions. But mostly it was farm animals. Then, after her dad and mom had divorced, and she'd gone away to live with her mom, her dad wrote to say he missed going to auctions with her. The last letter he wrote to her, after she'd grown up and was living with her husband, he said he'd bought a peach of a car at this auction for two hundred dollars. If she'd been there, he said, he'd have bought one for her, too. Three weeks later, in the middle of the night, a telephone call told her that he was dead. The car he'd bought leaked carbon monoxide up through the floorboards and caused him to pass out behind the wheel. He lived in the country. The motor went on running until there was no more gas in the tank. He stayed in the car until somebody found him a few days later.

The pan was starting to smoke. She poured in more oil and turned on the fan. She hadn't been to an auction in twenty years, and now she was getting ready to go to one tonight. But first she had to fry these pork chops. It was bad luck their fridge had gone flooey, but she found herself looking forward to this auction. She began missing her dad. She even missed her mom now, though the two of them used to argue all the time before she met her husband and began living with him. She stood at the stove, turning the meat, and missing both her dad and her mom.

Still missing them, she took a pot holder and moved the pan off the stove. Smoke was being drawn up through the vent over the stove. She stepped to the doorway with the pan and looked into the living room. The pan was still smoking and drops of oil and grease jumped over the sides as she held it. In the darkened room, she could just make out her husband's head, and his bare feet. "Come on out here," she said. "It's ready."

"Okay," he said. She saw his head come up from the end of the sofa. She put the pan back on the stove and turned to the cupboard. She took down a couple of plates and put them on the counter. She used her spatula to raise one of the pork chops. Then she lifted it onto a plate. The meat didn't look like meat. It looked like part of an old shoulder blade, or a digging instrument. But she knew it was a pork chop, and she took the other one out of the pan and put that on a plate, too.

In a minute, her husband came into the kitchen. He looked at the fridge once more, which was standing there with its door open. And then his eyes took in the pork chops. His mouth dropped open, but he didn't say anything. She waited for him to say something, anything, but he didn't. She put salt and pepper on the table and told him to sit down.

"Sit down," she said and gave him a plate on which lay the remains of a pork chop. "I want you to eat this," she said.

He took the plate. But he just stood there and looked at it. Then she turned to get her own plate.

Sandy cleared the newspaper away and shoved the food to the far side of the table. "Sit down," she said to her husband once more. He moved his plate from one hand to the other. But he kept standing there. It was then she saw puddles of water on the table. She heard water, too. It was dripping off the table and onto the linoleum.

She looked down at her husband's bare feet. She stared at his feet next to the pool of water. She knew she'd never again in her life see anything so unusual. But she didn't know what to make of it yet. She thought she'd better put on some lipstick, get her coat, and go ahead to the auction. But she couldn't take her eyes from her husband's feet. She put her plate on the table and watched until the feet left the kitchen and went back into the living room.

The Compartment

Myers was traveling through France in a first-class rail car on his way to visit his son in Strasbourg, who was a student at the university there. He hadn't seen the boy in eight years. There had been no phone calls between them during this time, not even a postcard since Myers and the boy's mother had gone their separate ways – the boy staying with her. The final break-up was hastened along, Myers always believed, by the boy's malign interference in their personal affairs.

The last time Myers had seen his son, the boy had lunged for him during a violent quarrel. Myers's wife had been standing by the sideboard, dropping one dish of china after the other onto the dining-room floor. Then she'd gone on to the cups. "That's enough," Myers had said, and at that instant the boy charged him. Myers side-stepped and got him in a headlock while the boy wept and pummeled Myers on the back and kidneys. Myers had him, and while he had him, he made the most of it. He slammed him into the wall and threatened to kill him. He meant it. "I gave you life," Myers remembered himself shouting, "and I can take it back!"

Thinking about that horrible scene now, Myers shook his head as if it had happened to someone else. And it had. He was simply not that same person. These days he lived alone and had little to do with anybody outside of his work. At night, he listened to classical music and read books on waterfowl decoys.

He lit a cigarette and continued to gaze out the train window, ignoring the man who sat in the seat next to the door and who slept with a hat pulled over his eyes. It was early in the morning and mist hung over the green fields that passed by outside. Now and then Myers saw a farmhouse and its outbuildings, everything surrounded by a wall. He thought this might be a good way to live – in an old house surrounded by a wall.

It was just past six o'clock. Myers hadn't slept since he'd boarded the train in Milan at eleven the night before. When the train had left Milan, he'd considered himself lucky to have the compartment to himself. He kept the light on and looked at guidebooks. He read things he wished he'd read before he'd been to the place they were about. He discovered much that he should have seen and done. In a way, he was sorry to be finding out certain things about the country now, just as he was leaving Italy behind after his first and, no doubt, last visit.

He put the guidebooks away in his suitcase, put the suitcase in the overhead rack, and took off his coat so he could use it for a blanket. He switched off the light and sat there in the darkened compartment with his eyes closed, hoping sleep would come.

After what seemed a long time, and just when he thought he was going to drop off, the train began to slow. It came to a stop at a little station outside of Basel. There, a middle-aged man in a dark suit, and wearing a hat, entered the compartment. The man said something to Myers in a language Myers didn't understand, and then the man put his leather bag up into the rack. He sat down on the other side of the compartment and straightened his shoulders. Then he pulled his hat over his eyes. By the time the train was moving again, the man was asleep and snoring quietly. Myers envied him.

In a few minutes, a Swiss official opened the door of the compartment and turned on the light. In English, and in some other language – German, Myers assumed – the official asked to see their passports. The man in the compartment with Myers pushed the hat back on his head, blinked his eyes, and reached into his coat pocket. The official studied the passport, looked at the man closely, and gave him back the document. Myers handed over his own passport. The official read the data, examined the photograph, and then looked at Myers before nodding and giving it back. He turned off the light as he went out. The man across from Myers pulled the hat over his eyes and put out his legs. Myers supposed he'd go right back to sleep, and once again he felt envy.

He stayed awake after that and began to think of the meeting with his son, which was now only a few hours away. How would he act when he saw the boy at the station? Should he embrace him? He felt uncomfortable with that prospect. Or should he merely offer his hand, smile as if these eight years had never occurred, and then pat the boy on the shoulder? Maybe the boy would say a few words – *I'm glad to see you – how was your trip?* And Myers would say – something. He really didn't know what he was going to say.

The French *contrôleur* walked by the compartment. He looked in on Myers and at the man sleeping across from Myers. This same *contrôleur* had already punched their tickets, so Myers turned his head and went back to looking out the window. More houses began to appear. But now there were no walls, and the houses were smaller and set closer together. Soon, Myers was sure, he'd see a French village. The haze was lifting. The train blew its whistle and sped past a crossing over which a barrier had been lowered. He saw a young woman with her hair pinned up and wearing a sweater, standing with her bicycle as she watched the cars whip past.

How's your mother? he might say to the boy after they had walked a little way from the station. *What do you hear from your mother?* For a wild instant, it occurred to Myers she could be dead. But then he understood that it couldn't be so, he'd have heard something – one way or the other, he'd have heard. He knew if he let himself go on thinking about these things, his heart could break. He closed the top button of his shirt and fixed his tie. He laid his coat across the seat next to him. He laced his shoes, got up, and stepped over the legs of the sleeping man. He let himself out of the compartment.

Myers had to put his hand against the windows along the corridor to steady himself as he moved toward the end of the car. He closed the door to the little toilet and locked it. Then he ran water and splashed his face. The train moved into a curve, still at the same high speed, and Myers had to hold on to the sink for balance.

The boy's letter had come to him a couple or months ago. The letter had been brief. He wrote that he'd been living in France and studying for the past year at the university in Strasbourg. There was no other information about what had possessed him to go to France, or what he'd been doing with himself during those years before France. Appropriately enough, Myers thought, no mention was made in the letter of the boy's mother – not a clue to her condition or where-abouts. But, inexplicably, the boy had closed the letter with the word Love, and Myers had pondered this for a long while. Finally, he'd answered the letter. After some delibera-tion, Myers wrote to say he had been thinking for some time of making a little trip to Europe. Would the boy like to meet him at the station in Strasbourg? He signed his letter, "Love,

Dad." He'd heard back from the boy and then he made his arrangements. It struck him that there was really no one, besides his secretary and a few business associates, that he felt it was necessary to tell he was going away. He had accumulated six weeks of vacation at the engineering firm where he worked, and he decided he would take all of the time coming to him for this trip. He was glad he'd done this, even though he now had no intention of spending all that time in Europe.

He'd gone first to Rome. But after the first few hours, walking around by himself on the streets, he was sorry he hadn't arranged to be with a group. He was lonely. He went to Venice, a city he and his wife had always talked of visiting. But Venice was a disappointment. He saw a man with one arm eating fried squid, and there were grimy, water-stained buildings everywhere he looked. He took a train to Milan, where he checked into a four-star hotel and spent the night watching a soccer match on a Sony color TV until the station went off the air. He got up the next morning and wandered around the city until it was time to go to the station. He'd planned the stopover in Strasbourg as the culmination of his trip. After a day or two, or three days – he'd see how it went – he would travel to Paris and fly home. He was tired of trying to make himself understood to strangers and would be glad to get back.

Someone tried the door to the WC. Myers finished tucking his shirt. He fastened his belt. Then he unlocked the door and, swaying with the movement of the train, walked back to his compartment. As he opened the door, he saw at once that his coat had been moved. It lay across a different seat from the one where he'd left it. He felt he had entered into a ludicrous but potentially serious situation. His heart began to race as he picked up the coat. He put his hand into the inside pocket and took out his passport. He carried his wallet in his hip pocket. So he still had his wallet and the passport. He went through the other coat pockets. What was missing was the gift he'd bought for the boy – an expensive Japanese wristwatch purchased at a shop in Rome. He had carried the watch in his inside coat pocket for safekeeping. Now the watch was gone.

"Pardon," he said to the man who slumped in the seat, legs out, the hat over his eyes. "Pardon." The man pushed the hat back and opened his eyes. He pulled himself up and looked at Myers. His eyes were large. He might have been dreaming. But he might not.

Myers said. "Did you see somebody come in here?"

But it was clear the man didn't know what Myers was saying. He continued to stare at him with what Myers took to be a look of total incomprehension. But maybe it was something else, Myers thought. Maybe the look masked slyness and deceit. Myers shook his coat to focus the man's attention. Then he put his hand into the pocket and rummaged. He pulled his sleeve back and showed the man his own wristwatch. The man looked at Myers and then at Myers's watch. He seemed mystified. Myers tapped the face of his watch. He put his other hand back into his coat pocket and made a gesture as if he were fishing for something. Myers pointed at the watch once more and waggled his fingers, hoping to signify the wristwatch taking flight out the door.

The man shrugged and shook his head.

"Goddamn it," Myers said in frustration. He put his coat on and went out into the corridor. He couldn't stay in the compartment another minute. He was afraid he might strike the man. He looked up and down the corridor, as if hoping he could see and recognize the thief. But there was no one around. Maybe the man who shared his compartment hadn't taken the watch. Maybe someone else, the person who tried the door to the WC, had walked past the compartment, spotted the coat and the sleeping man, and simply opened the door, gone through the pockets, closed the door, and gone away again.

Myers walked slowly to the end of the car, peering into the other compartments. It was not crowded in this first-class car, but there were one or two people in each compartment. Most of them were asleep, or seemed to be. Their eyes were closed, and their heads were thrown back against the seats. In one compartment, a man about his own age sat by the window looking out at the countryside. When Myers stopped at the glass and looked in at him, the man turned and regarded him fiercely.

Myers crossed into the second-class car. The compartments in this car were crowded – sometimes five or six passengers in each, and the people, he could tell at a glance, were more desperate. Many of them were awake – it was too uncomfortable to sleep – and they turned their eyes on him as he passed. Foreigners, he thought. It was clear to him that if the man in his compartment hadn't taken the watch, then the thief was from one of these compartments. But what could he do? It was hopeless. The watch was gone. It was in someone else's pocket now. He couldn't hope to make the *contrôleur* understand what had happened. And even if he could, then what? He made his way back to his own compartment. He looked in and saw that the man had stretched out again with his hat over his eyes.

Myers stepped over the man's legs and sat down in his seat by the window. He felt dazed with anger. They were on the outskirts of the city now. Farms and grazing land had given over to industrial plants with unpronounceable names on the fronts of the buildings. The train began slowing. Myers could see automobiles on city streets, and others waiting in line at the crossings for the train to pass. He got up and took his suitcase down. He held it on his lap while he looked out the window at this hateful place.

It came to him that he didn't want to see the boy after all. He was shocked by this realization and for a moment felt diminished by the meanness of it. He shook his head. In a lifetime of foolish actions, this trip was possibly the most foolish thing he'd ever done. But the fact was, he really had no desire to see this boy whose behavior had long ago isolated him from Myers's affections. He suddenly, and with great clarity, recalled the boy's face when he had lunged that time, and a wave of bitterness passed over Myers. This boy had devoured Myers's youth, had turned the young girl he had courted and wed into a nervous, alcoholic woman whom the boy alternately pitied and bullied. Why on earth, Myers asked himself, would he come all this way to see someone he disliked? He didn't want to shake the boy's hand, the hand of his enemy, nor have to clap him on the shoulder and make small-talk. He didn't want to have to ask him about his mother.

He sat forward in the seat as the train pulled into the station. An announcement was called out in French over the train's intercom. The man across from Myers began to stir. He adjusted his hat and sat up in the seat as something else in French came over the speaker. Myers didn't understand anything that was said. He grew more agitated as the train slowed and then came to a stop. He decided he wasn't going to leave the compartment. He was going to sit where he was until the train pulled away. When it did, he'd be on it, going on with the train to Paris, and that would be that. He looked out the window cautiously, afraid he'd see the boy's face at the glass. He didn't know what he'd do if that happened. He was afraid he might shake his fist. He saw a few people on the platform wearing coats and scarves who stood next to their suitcases, waiting to board the train. A few other people waited, without luggage, hands in their pockets, obviously expecting to meet someone. His son was not one of those waiting, but, of course, that didn't mean he wasn't out there somewhere. Myers moved the suitcase off his lap onto the floor and inched down in his seat.

The man across from him was yawning and looking out the window. Now he turned his gaze on Myers. He took off his hat and ran his hand through his hair. Then he put the hat back on, got to his feet, and pulled his bag down from the rack. He opened the compartment door. But before he went out, he turned around and gestured in the direction of the station.

"Strasbourg," the man said.

Myers turned away.

The man waited an instant longer, and then went out into the corridor with his bag and, Myers felt certain, with the wristwatch. But that was the least of his concerns now. He looked out the train window once again. He saw a man in an apron standing in the door of the station, smoking a cigarette. The man was watching two trainmen explaining something to a woman in a long skirt who held a baby in her arms. The woman listened and then nodded and listened some more. She moved the baby from one arm to the other. The men kept talking. She listened. One of the men chucked the baby under its chin. The woman looked down and smiled. She moved the baby again and listened some more. Myers saw a young couple embracing on the platform a little distance from his car. Then the young man let go of the young woman. He said something, picked up his valise, and moved to board the train. The woman watched him go.

She brought a hand up to her face, touched one eye and then the other with the heel of her hand. In a minute, Myers saw her moving down the platform, her eyes fixed on his car, as if following someone. He glanced away from the woman and looked at the big clock over the station's waiting room. He looked up and down the platform. The boy was nowhere in sight. It was possible he had overslept or it might be that he, too, had changed his mind. In any case, Myers felt relieved. He looked at the clock again, then at the young woman who was hurrying up to the window where he sat. Myers drew back as if she were going to strike the glass.

The door to the compartment opened. The young man he'd seen outside closed the door behind him and said, "*Bonjour.*" Without waiting for a reply, he threw his valise into the overhead rack and stepped over to the window. "*Pardonnez-moi.*" He pulled the window down. "Marie," he said. The young woman began to smile and cry at the same time. The young man brought her hands up and began kissing her fingers.

Myers looked away and clamped his teeth. He heard the final shouts of the trainmen. Someone blew a whistle. Presently, the train began to move away from the platform. The young man had let go of the woman's hands, but he continued to wave at her as the train rolled forward.

But the train went only a short distance, into the open air of the railyard, and then Myers felt it come to an abrupt stop. The young man closed the window and moved over to the seat by the door. He took a newspaper from his coat and began to read. Myers got up and opened the door. He went to the end of the corridor, where the cars were coupled together. He didn't know why they had stopped. Maybe something was wrong. He moved to the window. But all he could see was an intricate system of tracks where trains were being made up, cars taken off or switched from one train to another. He stepped back from the window. The sign on the door to the next car said, POUSSEZ. Myers struck the sign with his fist, and the door slid open. He was in the second-class car again. He passed along a row of compartments filled with people settling down, as if making ready for a long trip. He needed to find out from someone where this train was going. He had understood, at the time he purchased the ticket, that the train to Strasbourg went on to Paris. But he felt it would be humiliating to put his head into one of the compartments and say, "Paree?" or however they said it – as if asking if they'd arrived at a destination. He heard a loud clanking, and the train backed up a little. He could see the station again, and once more he thought of his son. Maybe he was standing back there, breathless from having rushed to get to the station, wondering what had happened to his father. Myers shook his head.

The car he was in creaked and groaned under him, then something caught and fell heavily into place. Myers looked out at the maze of tracks and realized that the train had begun to move again. He turned and hurried back to the end of the car and crossed back into the car he'd been traveling in. He walked down the corridor to his compartment. But the young man with the newspaper was gone. And Myers's suitcase was gone. It was not his compartment after all. He realized with a start they must have uncoupled his car while the train was in the yard and attached another second-class car to the train. The compartment he stood in front of was nearly filled with small, dark-skinned men who spoke rapidly in a language Myers had never heard before. One of the men signaled him to come inside. Myers moved into the compartment, and the men made room for him. There seemed to be a jovial air in the compartment. The man who'd signaled him laughed and parted the space next to him. Myers sat down with his back to the front of the train. The countryside out the window began to pass faster and faster. For a moment, Myers had the impression of the landscape shooting away from him. He was going somewhere, he knew that. And if it was the wrong direction, sooner or later he'd find it out.

He leaned against the seat and closed his eyes. The men went on talking and laughing. Their voices came to him as if from a distance. Soon the voices became part of the train's movements – and gradually Myers felt himself being carried, then pulled back, into sleep.

A Small, Good Thing

Saturday afternoon she drove to the bakery in the shopping center. After looking through a loose-leaf binder with photographs of cakes taped onto the pages, she ordered chocolate, the child's favorite. The cake she chose was decorated with a space ship and launching pad under a sprinkling of white stars, and a planet made of red frosting at the other end. His name, SCOTTY, would be in green letters beneath the planet. The baker, who was an older man with a thick neck, listened without saying anything when she told him the child would be eight years old next Monday. The baker wore a white apron that looked like a smock. Straps cut under his arms, went around in back and then to the front again, where they were secured under his heavy waist. He wiped his hands on his apron as he listened to her. He kept his eyes down on the photographs and let her talk. He let her take her time. He'd just come to work and he'd be there all night, baking, and he was in no real hurry.

She gave the baker her name, Ann Weiss, and her telephone number. The cake would be ready on Monday morning, just out of the oven, in plenty of time for the child's party that afternoon. The baker was not jolly. There were no pleasantries between them, just the minimum exchange of words, the necessary information. He made her feel uncomfortable, and she didn't like that. While he was bent over the counter with the pencil in his hand, she studied his coarse features and wondered if he'd ever done anything else with his life besides be a baker. She was a mother and thirty-three years old, and it seemed to her that everyone, especially someone the baker's age – a man old enough to be her father – must have children who'd gone through this special time of cakes and birthday parties. There must be that between them, she thought. But he was abrupt with her – not rude, just abrupt. She gave up trying to make friends with him. She looked into the back of the bakery and could see a long, heavy wooden table with aluminum pie pans stacked at one end; and beside the table a metal container filled with empty racks. There was an enormous oven. A radio was playing country-Western music.

The baker finished printing the information on the special order card and closed up the binder. He looked at her and said, "Monday morning." She thanked him and drove home.

On Monday morning, the birthday boy was walking to school with another boy. They were passing a bag of potato chips back and forth and the birthday boy was trying to find out what his friend intended to give him for his birthday that afternoon. Without looking, the birthday boy stepped off the curb at an intersection and was immediately knocked down by a car. He fell on his side with his head in the gutter and his legs out in the road. His eyes were closed, but his legs moved back and forth as if he were trying to climb over something. His friend dropped the potato chips and started to cry. The car had gone a hundred feet or so and stopped in the middle of the road. The man in the driver's seat looked back over his shoulder. He waited until the boy got unsteadily to his feet. The boy wobbled a little. He looked dazed, but okay. The driver put the car into gear and drove away.

The birthday boy didn't cry, but he didn't have anything

to say about anything either. He wouldn't answer when his friend asked him what it felt like to be hit by a car. He walked home, and his friend went on to school. But after the birthday boy was inside his house and was telling his mother about it — she sitting beside him on the sofa, holding his hands in her lap, saying, "Scotty, honey, are you sure you feel all right, baby?" thinking she would call the doctor anyway — he suddenly lay back on the sofa, closed his eyes, and went limp. When she couldn't wake him up, she hurried to the telephone and called her husband at work. Howard told her to remain calm, remain calm, and then he called an ambulance for the child and left for the hospital himself.

Of course, the birthday party was canceled. The child was in the hospital with a mild concussion and suffering from shock. There'd been vomiting, and his lungs had taken in fluid which needed pumping out that afternoon. Now he simply seemed to be in a very deep sleep — but no coma, Dr Francis had emphasized, no coma, when he saw the alarm in the parents' eyes. At eleven o'clock that night, when the boy seemed to be resting comfortably enough after the many X-rays and the lab work, and it was just a matter of his waking up and coming around, Howard left the hospital. He and Ann had been at the hospital with the child since that afternoon, and he was going home for a short while to bathe and change clothes. "I'll be back in an hour," he said. She nodded. "It's fine," she said. "I'll be right here." He kissed her on the forehead, and they touched hands. She sat in the chair beside the bed and looked at the child. She was waiting for him to wake up and be all right. Then she could begin to relax.

Howard drove home from the hospital. He took the wet, dark streets very fast, then caught himself and slowed down. Until now, his life had gone smoothly and to his satisfaction – college, marriage, another year of college for the advanced degree in business, a junior partnership in an investment firm. Fatherhood. He was happy and, so far, lucky – he knew that. His parents were still living, his brothers and his sister were established, his friends from college had gone out to take their places in the world. So far, he had kept away from any real harm, from those forces he knew existed and that could cripple or bring down a man if the luck went bad, if things suddenly turned. He pulled into the driveway and parked. His left leg began to tremble. He sat in the car for a minute and tried to deal with the present situation in a rational manner. Scotty had been hit by a car and was in the hospital, but he was going to be all right. Howard closed his eyes and ran his hand over his face. He got out of the car and went up to the front door. The dog was barking inside the house. The telephone rang and rang while he unlocked the door and fumbled for the light switch. He shouldn't have left the hospital, he shouldn't have. "Goddamn it!" he said. He picked up the receiver and said, "I just walked in the door!"

"There's a cake here that wasn't picked up," the voice on the other end of the line said.

"What are you saying?" Howard asked.

"A cake," the voice said. "A sixteen-dollar cake."

Howard held the receiver against his ear, trying to understand. "I don't know anything about a cake," he said. "Jesus, what are you talking about?"

"Don't hand me that," the voice said.

Howard hung up the telephone. He went into the kitchen and poured himself some whiskey. He called the hospital. But the child's condition remained the same; he was still sleeping and nothing had changed there. While water poured into the tub, Howard lathered his face and shaved. He'd just stretched out in the tub and closed his eyes when the telephone rang again. He hauled himself out, grabbed a towel, and hurried through the house, saying, "Stupid, stupid," for having left the hospital. But when he picked up the receiver and shouted, "Hello!" there was no sound at the other end of the line. Then the caller hung up.

He arrived back at the hospital a little after midnight. Ann still sat in the chair beside the bed. She looked up at Howard, and then she looked back at the child. The child's eyes stayed closed, the head was still wrapped in bandages. His breathing was quiet and regular. From an apparatus over the bed hung a bottle of glucose with a tube running from the bottle to the boy s arm.

"How is he?" Howard said. "What's all this?" waving at the glucose and the tube.

"Dr Francis's orders," she said. "He needs nourishment. He needs to keep up his strength. Why doesn't he wake up, Howard? I don't understand, if he's all right."

Howard put his hand against the back of her head. He ran his fingers through her hair. "He's going to be all right. He'll wake up in a little while. Dr Francis knows what's what."

After a time, he said, "Maybe you should go home and get some rest. I'll stay here. Just don't put up with this creep who keeps calling. Hang up right away."

"Who's calling?" she asked.

"I don't know who, just somebody with nothing better to do than call up people. You go on now."

She shook her head. "No," she said, "I'm fine."

"Really," he said. "Go home for a while, and then come back and spell me in the morning. It'll be all right. What did Dr Francis say? He said Scotty's going to be all right. We don't have to worry. He's just sleeping now, that's all."

A nurse pushed the door open. She nodded at them as she went to the bedside. She took the left arm out from under the covers and put her fingers on the wrist, found the pulse, then consulted her watch. In a little while, she put the arm back under the covers and moved to the foot of the bed, where she wrote something on a clipboard attached to the bed.

"How is he?" Ann said. Howard's hand was a weight on her shoulder. She was aware of the pressure from his fingers.

"He's stable," the nurse said. Then she said, "Doctor will be in again shortly. Doctor's back in the hospital. He's making rounds right now."

"I was saying maybe she'd want to go home and get a little rest," Howard said. "After the doctor comes," he said.

"She could do that," the nurse said. "I think you should both feel free to do that, if you wish." The nurse was a big Scandinavian woman with blond hair. There was the trace of an accent in her speech.

"We'll see what the doctor says," Ann said. "I want to talk to the doctor. I don't think he should keep sleeping like this. I don't think that's a good sign." She brought her hand up to her eyes and let her head come forward a little. Howard's grip tightened on her shoulder, and then his hand moved up to her neck, where his fingers began to knead the muscles there.

"Dr Francis will be here in a few minutes," the nurse said. Then she left the room.

Howard gazed at his son for a time, the small chest quietly rising and falling under the covers. For the first time since the terrible minutes after Ann's telephone call to him at his office, he felt a genuine fear starting in his limbs. He began shaking his head. Scotty was fine, but instead of sleeping at home in his own bed, he was in a hospital bed with bandages around his head and a tube in his arm. But this help was what he needed right now.

Dr Francis came in and shook hands with Howard, though they'd just seen each other a few hours before. Ann got up from the chair. "Doctor?"

"Ann," he said and nodded. "Let's just first see how he's doing," the doctor said. He moved to the side of the bed and took the boy's pulse. He peeled back one eyelid and then the other. Howard and Ann stood beside the doctor and watched. Then the doctor turned back the covers and listened to the boy's heart and lungs with his stethoscope. He pressed his fingers here and there on the abdomen. When he was finished, he went to the end of the bed and studied the chart. He noted the time, scribbled something on the chart, and then looked at Howard and Ann.

"Doctor, how is he?" Howard said. "What's the matter with him exactly?"

"Why doesn't he wake up?" Ann said.

The doctor was a handsome, big-shouldered man with a tanned face. He wore a three-piece blue suit, a striped tie, and ivory cufflinks. His gray hair was combed along the sides of his head, and he looked as if he had just come from a concert. "He's all right," the doctor said. "Nothing to shout about, he could be better, I think. But he's all right. Still, I wish he'd wake up. He should wake up pretty soon." The doctor looked at the boy again. "We'll know some more in a couple of hours, after the results of a few more tests are in. But he's all right, believe me, except for the hairline fracture of the skull. He does have that."

"Oh, no," Ann said.

"And a bit of a concussion, as I said before. Of course, you know he's in shock," the doctor said. "Sometimes you see this in shock cases. This sleeping."

"But he's out of any real danger?" Howard said. "You said before he's not in a coma. You wouldn't call this a coma, then – would you, doctor?" Howard waited. He looked at the doctor.

"No, I don't want to call it a coma," the doctor said and glanced over at the boy once more. "He's just in a very deep sleep. It's a restorative measure the body is taking on its own. He's out of any real danger, I'd say that for certain, yes. But we'll know more when he wakes up and the other tests are in," the doctor said.

"It's a coma," Ann said. "Of sorts."

"It's not a coma yet, not exactly," the doctor said. "I wouldn't want to call it coma. Not yet, anyway. He's suffered shock. In shock cases, this kind of reaction is common enough; it's a temporary reaction to bodily trauma. Coma. Well, coma is a deep, prolonged unconsciousness, something that could go on for days, or weeks even. Scotty's not in that area, not as far as we can tell. I'm certain his condition will show improvement by morning. I'm betting that it will. We'll know more when he wakes up, which shouldn't be long now. Of course, you may do as you like, stay here or go home for a time. But by all means feel free to leave the hospital for a while if you want. This is not easy, I know." The doctor gazed at the boy again, watching him, and then he turned to Ann and said, "You try not to worry, little mother. Believe me, we're doing all that can be done. It's just a question of a little more time now." He nodded at her, shook hands with Howard again, and then he left the room.

Ann put her hand over the child's forehead. "At least he doesn't have a fever," she said. Then she said, "My God, he feels so cold, though. Howard? Is he supposed to feel like this? Feel his head."

Howard touched the child's temples. His own breathing

had slowed. "I think he's supposed to feel this way right now," he said. "He's in shock, remember? That's what the doctor said. The doctor was just in here. He would have said something if Scotty wasn't okay."

Ann stood there a while longer, working her lip with her teeth. Then she moved over to her chair and sat down.

Howard sat in the chair next to her chair. They looked at each other. He wanted to say something else and reassure her, but he was afraid, too. He took her hand and put it in his lap, and this made him feel better, her hand being there. He picked up her hand and squeezed it. Then he just held her hand. They sat like that for a while, watching the boy and not talking. From time to time, he squeezed her hand. Finally, she took her hand away.

"I've been praying," she said.

He nodded.

She said, "I almost thought I'd forgotten how, but it came back to me. All I had to do was close my eyes and say, 'Please God, help us – help Scotty,' and then the rest was easy. The words were right there. Maybe if you prayed, too," she said to him.

"I've already prayed," he said. "I prayed this afternoon – yesterday afternoon, I mean – after you called, while I was driving to the hospital. I've been praying," he said.

"That's good," she said. For the first time, she felt they were together in it, this trouble. She realized with a start that, until now, it had only been happening to her and to Scotty. She hadn't let Howard into it, though he was there and needed all along. She felt glad to be his wife.

The same nurse came in and took the boy's pulse again and checked the flow from the bottle hanging above the bed.

In an hour, another doctor came in. He said his name was Parsons, from Radiology. He had a bushy mustache.

He was wearing loafers, a Western shirt, and a pair of jeans.

"We're going to take him downstairs for more pictures," he told them. "We need to do some more pictures, and we want to do a scan."

"What's that?" Ann said. "A scan?" She stood between this new doctor and the bed. "I thought you'd already taken all your X-rays."

"I'm afraid we need some more," he said. "Nothing to be alarmed about. We just need some more pictures, and we want to do a brain scan on him."

"My God," Ann said.

"It's perfectly normal procedure in cases like this," this new doctor said. "We just need to find out for sure why he isn't back awake yet. It's normal medical procedure, and nothing to be alarmed about. We'll be taking him down in a few minutes," this doctor said.

In a little while, two orderlies came into the room with a gurney. They were black-haired, dark-complexioned men in white uniforms, and they said a few words to each other in a foreign tongue as they unhooked the boy from the tube and moved him from his bed to the gurney. Then they wheeled him from the room. Howard and Ann got on the same elevator. Ann gazed at the child. She closed her eyes as the elevator began its descent. The orderlies stood at either end of the gurney without saying anything, though once one of the men made a comment to the other in their own language, and the other man nodded slowly in response.

Later that morning, just as the sun was beginning to lighten the windows in the waiting room outside the X-ray department, they brought the boy out and moved him back up to his room. Howard and Ann rode up on the elevator with him once more, and once more they took up their places beside the bed.

* * *

They waited all day, but still the boy did not wake up. Occasionally, one of them would leave the room to go downstairs to the cafeteria to drink coffee and then, as if suddenly remembering and feeling guilty, get up from the table and hurry back to the room. Dr Francis came again that afternoon and examined the boy once more and then left after telling them he was coming along and could wake up at any minute now. Nurses, different nurses from the night before, came in from time to time. Then a young woman from the lab knocked and entered the room. She wore white slacks and a white blouse and carried a little tray of things which she put on the stand beside the bed. Without a word to them, she took blood from the boy's arm. Howard closed his eyes as the woman found the right place on the boy's arm and pushed the needle in.

"I don't understand this," Ann said to the woman.

"Doctor's orders," the young woman said. "I do what I'm told. They say draw that one, I draw. What's wrong with him, anyway?" she said. "He's a sweetie."

"He was hit by a car," Howard said. "A hit-and-run."

The young woman shook her head and looked again at the boy. Then she took her tray and left the room.

"Why won't he wake up?" Ann said. "Howard? I want some answers from these people."

Howard didn't say anything. He sat down again in the chair and crossed one leg over the other. He rubbed his face. He looked at his son and then he settled back in the chair, closed his eyes, and went to sleep.

Ann walked to the window and looked out at the parking lot. It was night, and cars were driving into and out of the parking lot with their lights on. She stood at the window with her hands gripping the sill, and knew in her heart that they were into something now, something hard. She was afraid, and her teeth began to chatter until she tightened her jaws. She saw a big car stop in front of the hospital and someone, a woman in a long coat, get into the car. She wished she were that woman and somebody, anybody, was driving her away from here to somewhere else, a place where she would find Scotty waiting for her when she stepped out of the car, ready to say Mom and let her gather him in her arms.

In a little while, Howard woke up. He looked at the boy again. Then he got up from the chair, stretched, and went over to stand beside her at the window. They both stared out at the parking lot. They didn't say anything. But they seemed to feel each other's insides now, as though the worry had made them transparent in a perfectly natural way.

The door opened and Dr Francis came in. He was wearing a different suit and tie this time. His gray hair was combed along the sides of his head, and he looked as if he had just shaved. He went straight to the bed and examined the boy. "He ought to have come around by now. There's just no good reason for this," he said. "But I can tell you we're all convinced he's out of any danger. We'll just feel better when he wakes up. There's no reason, absolutely none, why he shouldn't come around. Very soon. Oh, he'll have himself a dilly of a headache when he does, you can count on that. But all of his signs are fine. They're as normal as can be."

"It is a coma, then?" Ann said.

The doctor rubbed his smooth cheek. "We'll call it that for the time being, until he wakes up. But you must be worn out. This is hard. I know this is hard. Feel free to go out for a bite," he said. "It would do you good. I'll put a nurse in here while you're gone if you'll feel better about going. Go and have yourselves something to eat."

"I couldn't eat anything," Ann said.

"Do what you need to do, of course," the doctor said. "Anyway, I wanted to tell you that all the signs are good, the tests are negative, nothing showed up at all, and just as soon as he wakes up he'll be over the hill."

"Thank you, doctor," Howard said. He shook hands with the doctor again. The doctor patted Howard's shoulder and went out.

"I suppose one of us should go home and check on things," Howard said. "Slug needs to be fed, for one thing."

"Call one of the neighbors," Ann said. "Call the Morgans. Anyone will feed a dog if you ask them to."

"All right," Howard said. After a while, he said, "Honey, why don't you do it? Why don't *you* go home and check on things, and then come back? It'll do you good. I'll be right here with him. Seriously," he said. "We need to keep up our strength on this. We'll want to be here for a while even after he wakes up."

"Why don't *you* go?" she said. "Feed Slug. Feed yourself."

"I already went," he said. "I was gone for exactly an hour and fifteen minutes. You go home for an hour and freshen up. Then come back."

She tried to think about it, but she was too tired. She closed her eyes and tried to think about it again. After a time, she said, "Maybe I *will* go home for a few minutes. Maybe if I'm not just sitting right here watching him every second, he'll wake up and be all right. You know? Maybe he'll wake up if I'm not here. I'll go home and take a bath and put on clean clothes. I'll feed Slug. Then I'll come back."

"I'll be right here," he said. "You go on home, honey. I'll keep an eye on things here." His eyes were bloodshot and small, as if he'd been drinking for a long time. His clothes were rumpled. His beard had come out again. She touched his face, and then she took her hand back. She understood he wanted to be by himself for a while, not have to talk or share his worry for a time. She picked her purse up from the nightstand; and he helped her into her coat.

"I won't be gone long," she said.

"Just sit and rest for a little while when you get home," he said. "Eat something. Take a bath. After you get out of the bath, just sit for a while and rest. It'll do you a world of good, you'll see. Then come back," he said. "Let's try not to worry. You heard what Dr Francis said."

She stood in her coat for a minute trying to recall the doctor's exact words, looking for any nuances, any hint of something behind his words other than what he had said. She tried to remember if his expression had changed any when he bent over to examine the child. She remembered the way his features had composed themselves as he rolled back the child's eyelids and then listened to his breathing.

She went to the door, where she turned and looked back. She looked at the child, and then she looked at the father. Howard nodded. She stepped out of the room and pulled the door closed behind her.

She went past the nurses' station and down to the end of the corridor, looking for the elevator. At the end of the corridor, she turned to her right and entered a little waiting room where a Negro family sat in wicker chairs. There was a middle-aged man in a khaki shirt and pants, a baseball cap pushed back on his head. A large woman wearing a house-dress and slippers was slumped in one of the chairs. A teenaged girl in jeans, hair done in dozens of little braids, lay stretched out in one of the chairs smoking a cigarette, her legs crossed at the ankles. The family swung their eyes to Ann as she entered the room. The little table was littered with hamburger wrappers and Styrofoam cups.

"Franklin," the large woman said as she roused herself. "Is it about Franklin?" Her eyes widened. "Tell me now, lady," the woman said. "Is it about Franklin?" She was trying to rise from her chair, but the man had closed his hand over her arm.

"Here, here," he said. "Evelyn."

"I'm sorry," Ann said. "I'm looking for the elevator. My son is in the hospital, and now I can't find the elevator."

"Elevator is down that way, turn left," the man said as he aimed a finger.

The girl drew on her cigarette and stared at Ann. Her eyes were narrowed to slits, and her broad lips parted slowly as she let the smoke escape. The Negro woman let her head fall on her shoulder and looked away from Ann, no longer interested.

"My son was hit by a car," Ann said to the man. She seemed to need to explain herself. "He has a concussion and a little skull fracture, but he's going to be all right. He's in shock now, but it might be some kind of coma, too. That's what really worries us, the coma part. I'm going out for a little while, but my husband is with him. Maybe he'll wake up while I'm gone."

"That's too bad," the man said and shifted in the chair. He shook his head. He looked down at the table, and then he looked back at Ann. She was still standing there. He said, "Our Franklin, he's on the operating table. Somebody cut him. Tried to kill him. There was a fight where he was at. At this party. They say he was just standing and watching. Not bothering nobody. But that don't mean nothing these days. Now he's on the operating table. We're just hoping and praying, that's all we can do now." He gazed at her steadily.

Ann looked at the girl again, who was still watching her, and at the older woman, who kept her head down, but whose eyes were now closed. Ann saw the lips moving silently, making words. She had an urge to ask what those words were. She wanted to talk more with these people who were in the same kind of waiting she was in. She was afraid, and they were afraid. They had that in common. She would have liked to have said something else about the accident, told them more about Scotty, that it had happened on the day of his birthday, Monday, and that he was still unconscious. Yet she didn't know how to begin. She stood looking at them without saying anything more.

She went down the corridor the man had indicated and found the elevator. She waited a minute in front of the closed doors, still wondering if she was doing the right thing. Then she put out her finger and touched the button.

She pulled into the driveway and cut the engine. She closed her eyes and leaned her head against the wheel for a minute. She listened to the ticking sounds the engine made as it began to cool. Then she got out of the car. She could hear the dog barking inside the house. She went to the front door, which was unlocked. She went inside and turned on lights and put on a kettle of water for tea. She opened some dogfood and fed Slug on the back porch. The dog ate in hungry little smacks. It kept running into the kitchen to see that she was going to stay. As she sat down on the sofa with her tea, the telephone rang.

"Yes!" she said as she answered. "Hello!"

"Mrs Weiss," a man's voice said. It was five o'clock in the morning, and she thought she could hear machinery or equipment of some kind in the background.

"Yes, yes! What is it?" she said. "This is Mrs Weiss. This is she. What is it, please?" She listened to whatever it was in the background. "Is it Scotty, for Christ's sake?"

"Scotty," the man's voice said. "It's about Scotty, yes. It has to do with Scotty, that problem. Have you forgotten about Scotty?" the man said. Then he hung up.

She dialled the hospital's number and asked for the third floor. She demanded information about her son from the nurse who answered the telephone. Then she asked to speak to her husband. It was, she said, an emergency.

She waited, turning the telephone cord in her fingers. She closed her eyes and felt sick at her stomach. She would have to make herself eat. Slug came in from the back porch and lay down near her feet. He wagged his tail. She pulled at his ear while he licked her fingers. Howard was on the line.

"Somebody just called here," she said. She twisted the telephone cord. "He said it was about Scotty," she cried.

"Scotty's fine," Howard told her. "I mean, he's still sleeping. There's been no change. The nurse has been in twice since you've been gone. A nurse or else a doctor. He's all right."

"This man called. He said it was about Scotty," she told him.

"Honey, you rest for a little while, you need the rest. It must be that same caller I had. Just forget it. Come back down here after you've rested. Then we'll have breakfast or something."

"Breakfast," she said. "I don't want any breakfast."

"You know what I mean," he said. "Juice, something. I don't know. I don't know anything, Ann. Jesus, I'm not hungry, either. Ann, it's hard to talk now. I'm standing here at the desk. Dr Francis is coming again at eight o'clock this morning. He's going to have something to tell us then, something more definite. That's what one of the nurses said. She didn't know any more than that. Ann? Honey, maybe we'll know something more then. At eight o'clock. Come back here before eight. Meanwhile, I'm right here and Scotty's all right. He's still the same," he added.

"I was drinking a cup of tea," she said, "when the telephone rang. They said it was about Scotty. There was a noise in the background. Was there a noise in the background on that call you had, Howard?"

"I don't remember," he said. "Maybe the driver of the car, maybe he's a psychopath and found out about Scotty somehow. But I'm here with him. Just rest like you were going to do. Take a bath and come back by seven or so, and we'll talk to the doctor together when he gets here. It's going to be all right, honey. I'm here, and there are doctors and nurses around. They say his condition is stable."

"I'm scared to death," she said.

She ran water, undressed, and got into the tub. She washed and dried quickly, not taking the time to wash her hair. She put on clean underwear, wool slacks, and a sweater. She went into the living room, where the dog looked up at her and let its tail thump once against the floor. It was just starting to get light outside when she went out to the car.

She drove into the parking lot of the hospital and found a space close to the front door. She felt she was in some obscure way responsible for what had happened to the child. She let her thoughts move to the Negro family. She remembered the name Franklin and the table that was covered with hamburger papers, and the teenaged girl staring at her as she drew on her cigarette. "Don't have children," she told the girl's image as she entered the front door of the hospital. "For God's sake, don't."

She took the elevator up to the third floor with two nurses who were just going on duty. It was Wednesday morning, a few minutes before seven. There was a page for a Dr Madison as the elevator doors slid open on the third floor. She got off behind the nurses, who turned in the other direction and continued the conversation she had interrupted when she'd gotten into the elevator. She walked down the corridor to the little alcove where the Negro family had been waiting. They were gone now, but the chairs were scattered in such a way that it looked as if people had just jumped up from them the minute before. The tabletop was cluttered with the same cups and papers, the ashtray was filled with cigarette butts.

She stopped at the nurses' station. A nurse was standing behind the counter, brushing her hair and yawning.

"There was a Negro boy in surgery last night," Ann said. "Franklin was his name. His family was in the waiting room. I'd like to inquire about his condition."

A nurse who was sitting at a desk behind the counter looked up from a chart in front of her. The telephone buzzed and she picked up the receiver, but she kept her eyes on Ann.

"He passed away," said the nurse at the counter. The nurse held the hairbrush and kept looking at her. "Are you a friend of the family or what?"

"I met the family last night," Ann said. "My own son is in the hospital. I guess he's in shock. We don't know for sure what's wrong. I just wondered about Franklin, that's all. Thank you." She moved down the corridor. Elevator doors the same color as the walls slid open and a gaunt, bald man in white pants and white canvas shoes pulled a heavy cart off the elevator. She hadn't noticed these doors last night. The man wheeled the cart out into the corridor and stopped in front of the room nearest the elevator and consulted a clipboard. Then he reached down and slid a tray out of the cart. He rapped lightly on the door and entered the room. She could smell the unpleasant odors of warm food as she passed the cart. She hurried on without looking at any of the nurses and pushed open the door to the child's room.

Howard was standing at the window with his hands behind

his back. He turned around as she came in.

"How is he?" she said. She went over to the bed. She dropped her purse on the floor beside the nightstand. It seemed to her she had been gone a long time. She touched the child's face. "Howard?"

"Dr Francis was here a little while ago," Howard said. She looked at him closely and thought his shoulders were bunched a little.

"I thought he wasn't coming until eight o'clock this morning," she said quickly.

"There was another doctor with him. A neurologist."

"A neurologist," she said.

Howard nodded. His shoulders were bunching, she could see that. "What'd they say, Howard? For Christ's sake, what'd they say? What is it?"

"They said they're going to take him down and run more tests on him, Ann. They think they're going to operate, honey. Honey, they *are* going to operate. They can't figure out why he won't wake up. It's more than just shock or concussion, they know that much now. It's in his skull, the fracture, it has something, something to do with that, they think. So they're going to operate. I tried to call you, but I guess you'd already left the house."

"Oh, God," she said. "Oh, please, Howard, please," she said, taking his arms.

"Look!" Howard said. "Scotty! Look, Ann!" He turned her toward the bed.

The boy had opened his eyes, then closed them. He opened them again now. The eyes stared straight ahead for a minute, then moved slowly in his head until they rested on Howard and Ann, then traveled away again.

"Scotty," his mother said, moving to the bed.

"Hey, Scott," his father said. "Hey, son."

74

They leaned over the bed. Howard took the child's hand in his hands and began to pat and squeeze the hand. Ann bent over the boy and kissed his forehead again and again. She put her hands on either side of his face. "Scotty, honey, it's Mommy and Daddy," she said. "Scotty?"

The boy looked at them, but without any sign of recognition. Then his mouth opened, his eyes scrunched closed, and he howled until he had no more air in his lungs. His face seemed to relax and soften then. His lips parted as his last breath was puffed through his throat and exhaled gently through the clenched teeth.

The doctors called it a hidden occlusion and said it was a one-in-a-million circumstance. Maybe if it could have been detected somehow and surgery undertaken immediately, they could have saved him. But more than likely not. In any case, what would they have been looking for? Nothing had shown up in the tests or in the X-rays.

Dr Francis was shaken. "I can't tell you how badly I feel. I'm so very sorry, I can't tell you," he said as he led them into the doctors' lounge. There was a doctor sitting in a chair with his legs hooked over the back of another chair, watching an early-morning TV show. He was wearing a green delivery-room outfit, loose green pants and green blouse, and a green cap that covered his hair. He looked at Howard and Ann and then looked at Dr Francis. He got to his feet and turned off the set and went out of the room. Dr Francis guided Ann to the sofa, sat down beside her, and began to talk in a low, consoling voice. At one point, he leaned over and embraced her. She could feel his chest rising and falling evenly against her shoulder. She kept her eyes open and let him hold her. Howard went into the bathroom, but he left the door open. After a violent fit of weeping, he ran water and washed his face. Then he came out and sat down at the little table that held a telephone. He looked at the telephone as though deciding what to do first. He made some calls. After a time, Dr Francis used the telephone.

"Is there anything else I can do for the moment?" he asked them.

Howard shook his head. Ann stared at Dr Francis as if unable to comprehend his words.

The doctor walked them to the hospital's front door. People were entering and leaving the hospital. It was eleven o'clock in the morning. Ann was aware of how slowly, almost reluctantly, she moved her feet. It seemed to her that Dr Francis was making them leave when she felt they should stay, when it would be more the right thing to do to stay. She gazed out into the parking lot and then turned around and looked back at the front of the hospital. She began shaking her head. "No, no," she said. "I can't leave him here, no." She heard herself say that and thought how unfair it was that the only words that came out were the sort of words used on TV shows where people were stunned by violent or sudden deaths. She wanted her words to be her own. "No," she said, and for some reason the memory of the Negro woman's head lolling on the woman's shoulder came to her. "No," she said again.

"I'll be talking to you later in the day," the doctor was saying to Howard. "There are still some things that have to be done, things that have to be cleared up to our satisfaction. Some things that need explaining."

"An autopsy," Howard said.

Dr Francis nodded.

"I understand," Howard said. Then he said, "Oh, Jesus. No, I don't understand, doctor. I can't, I can't. I just can't."

Dr Francis put his arm around Howard's shoulders. "I'm

sorry. God, how I'm sorry." He let go of Howard's shoulders and held out his hand. Howard looked at the hand, and then he took it. Dr Francis put his arms around Ann once more. He seemed full of some goodness she didn't understand. She let her head rest on his shoulder, but her eyes stayed open. She kept looking at the hospital. As they drove out of the parking lot, she looked back at the hospital.

At home, she sat on the sofa with her hands in her coat pockets. Howard closed the door to the child's room. He got the coffee-maker going and then he found an empty box. He had thought to pick up some of the child's things that were scattered around the living room. But instead he sat down beside her on the sofa, pushed the box to one side, and leaned forward, arms between his knees. He began to weep. She pulled his head over into her lap and patted his shoulder. "He's gone," she said. She kept patting his shoulder. Over his sobs, she could hear the coffee-maker hissing in the kitchen. "There, there," she said tenderly. "Howard, he's gone. He's gone and now we'll have to get used to that. To being alone."

In a little while, Howard got up and began moving aimlessly around the room with the box, not putting anything into it, but collecting some things together on the floor at one end of the sofa. She continued to sit with her hands in her coat pockets. Howard put the box down and brought coffee into the living room. Later, Ann made calls to relatives. After each call had been placed and the party had answered, Ann would blurt out a few words and cry for a minute. Then she would quietly explain, in a measured voice, what had happened and tell them about arrangements. Howard took the box out to the garage, where he saw the child's bicycle. He dropped the box and sat down on the pavement beside the bicycle. He took hold of the bicycle awkwardly so that it leaned against his chest. He held it, the rubber pedal sticking into his chest. He gave the wheel a turn.

Ann hung up the telephone after talking to her sister. She was looking up another number when the telephone rang. She picked it up on the first ring.

"Hello," she said, and she heard something in the background, a humming noise. "Hello!" she said. "For God's sake," she said. "Who is this? What is it you want?"

"Your Scotty, I got him ready for you," the man's voice said. "Did you forget him?"

"You evil bastard!" she shouted into the receiver. "How can you do this, you evil son of a bitch?"

"Scotty," the man said. "Have you forgotten about Scotty?" Then the man hung up on her.

Howard heard the shouting and came in to find her with her head on her arms over the table, weeping. He picked up the receiver and listened to the dial tone.

Much later, just before midnight, after they had dealt with many things, the telephone rang again.

"You answer it," she said. "Howard, it's him, I know." They were sitting at the kitchen table with coffee in front of them. Howard had a small glass of whiskey beside his cup. He answered on the third ring.

"Hello," he said. "Who is this? Hello! Hello!" The line went dead. "He hung up," Howard said. "Whoever it was."

"It was him," she said. "That bastard. I'd like to kill him," she said. "I'd like to shoot him and watch him kick," she said.

"Ann, my God," he said.

"Could you hear anything?" she said. "In the background? A noise, machinery, something humming?"

"Nothing, really. Nothing like that," he said. "There wasn't much time. I think there was some radio music. Yes, there was a radio going, that's all I could tell. I don't know what in God's name is going on," he said.

She shook her head. "If I could, could get my hands on him." It came to her then. She knew who it was. Scotty, the cake, the telephone number. She pushed the chair away from the table and got up. "Drive me down to the shopping center," she said. "Howard."

"What are you saying?"

"The shopping center. I know who it is who's calling. I know who it is. It's the baker, the son-of-a-bitching baker, Howard. I had him bake a cake for Scotty's birthday. That's who's calling. That's who has the number and keeps calling us. To harass us about that cake. The baker, that bastard."

They drove down to the shopping center. The sky was clear and stars were out. It was cold, and they ran the heater in the car. They parked in front of the bakery. All of the shops and stores were closed, but there were cars at the far end of the lot in front of the movie theater. The bakery windows were dark, but when they looked through the glass they could see a light in the back room and, now and then, a big man in an apron moving in and out of the white, even light. Through the glass, she could see the display cases and some little tables with chairs She tried the door. She rapped on the glass. But if the baker heard them, he gave no sign. He didn't look in their direction.

They drove around behind the bakery and parked. They got out of the car. There was a lighted window too high up for them to see inside. A sign near the back door said THE PANTRY BAKERY, SPECIAL ORDERS. She could hear faintly a radio playing inside and something creak – an oven door as it was pulled down? She knocked on the door and waited. Then she knocked again, louder. The radio was turned down and there was a scraping sound now, the distinct sound of something, a drawer, being pulled open and then closed.

Someone unlocked the door and opened it. The baker stood in the light and peered out at them. "I'm closed for business," he said. "What do you want at this hour? It's midnight. Are you drunk or something?"

She stepped into the light that fell through the open door. He blinked his heavy eyelids as he recognized her. "It's you," he said.

"It's me," she said. "Scotty's mother. This is Scotty's father. We'd like to come in."

The baker said, "I'm busy now. I have work to do."

She had stepped inside the doorway anyway. Howard came in behind her. The baker moved back. "It smells like a bakery in here. Doesn't it smell like a bakery in here, Howard?"

"What do you want?" the baker said. "Maybe you want your cake? That's it, you decided you want your cake. You ordered a cake, didn't you?"

"You're pretty smart for a baker," she said. "Howard, this is the man who's been calling us." She clenched her fists. She stared at him fiercely. There was a deep burning inside her, an anger that made her feel larger than herself, larger than either of these men.

"Just a minute here," the baker said. "You want to pick up your three-day-old cake? That it? I don't want to argue with you, lady. There it sits over there, getting stale. I'll give it to you for half of what I quoted you. No. You want it? You can have it. It's no good to me, no good to anyone now. It cost me time and money to make that cake. If you want it, okay, if you don't, that's okay, too. I have to get back to work." He looked at them and rolled his tongue behind his teeth.

"More cakes," she said. She knew she was in control of it, of what was increasing in her. She was calm.

"Lady, I work sixteen hours a day in this place to earn a living," the baker said. He wiped his hands on his apron. "I work night and day in here, trying to make ends meet." A look crossed Ann's face that made the baker move back and say, "No trouble, now." He reached to the counter and picked up a rolling pin with his right hand and began to tap it against the palm of his other hand. "You want the cake or not? I have to get back to work. Bakers work at night," he said again. His eyes were small, mean-looking, she thought, nearly lost in the bristly flesh around his cheeks. His neck was thick with fat.

"I know bakers work at night," Ann said. "They make phone calls at night, too. You bastard," she said.

The baker continued to tap the rolling pin against his hand. He glanced at Howard. "Careful, careful," he said to Howard.

"My son's dead," she said with a cold, even finality. "He was hit by a car Monday morning. We've been waiting with him until he died. But, of course, you couldn't be expected to know that, could you? Bakers can't know everything – can they, Mr Baker? But he's dead. He's dead, you bastard!" Just as suddenly as it had welled in her, the anger dwindled, gave way to something else, a dizzy feeling of nausea. She leaned against the wooden table that was sprinkled with flour, put her hands over her face, and began to cry, her shoulders rocking back and forth. "It isn't fair," she said. "It isn't, isn't fair."

Howard put his hand at the small of her back and looked at the baker. "Shame on you," Howard said to him. "Shame."

The baker put the rolling pin back on the counter. He undid his apron and threw it on the counter. He looked at them, and then he shook his head slowly. He pulled a chair out from under the card table that held papers and receipts, an adding machine, and a telephone directory. "Please sit down," he said. "Let me get you a chair," he said to Howard. "Sit down now, please." The baker went into the front of the shop and returned with two little wrought-iron chairs. "Please sit down, you people."

Ann wiped her eyes and looked at the baker. "I wanted to kill you," she said. "I wanted you dead."

The baker had cleared a space for them at the table. He shoved the adding machine to one side, along with the stacks of notepaper and receipts. He pushed the telephone directory onto the floor, where it landed with a thud. Howard and Ann sat down and pulled their chairs up to the table. The baker sat down, too.

"Let me say how sorry I am," the baker said, putting his elbows on the table. "God alone knows how sorry. Listen to me. I'm just a baker. I don't claim to be anything else. Maybe once, maybe years ago, I was a different kind of human being. I've forgotten, I don't know for sure. But I'm not any longer, if I ever was. Now I'm just a baker. That don't excuse my doing what I did, I know. But I'm deeply sorry. I'm sorry for your son, and sorry for my part in this," the baker said. He spread his hands out on the table and turned them over to reveal his palms. "I don't have any children myself, so I can only imagine what you must be feeling. All I can say to you now is that I'm sorry. Forgive me, if you can," the baker said. "I'm not an evil man, I don't think. Not evil, like you said on the phone. You got to understand what it comes down to is I don't know how to act anymore, it would seem. Please," the man said, "let me ask you if you can find it in your hearts to forgive me?"

It was warm inside the bakery. Howard stood up from the table and took off his coat. He helped Ann from her coat. The baker looked at them for a minute and then nodded and got up from the table. He went to the oven and turned off some switches. He found cups and poured coffee from an electric coffee-maker. He put a carton of cream on the table, and a bowl of sugar.

"You probably need to eat something," the baker said. "I hope you'll eat some of my hot rolls. You have to eat and keep going. Eating is a small, good thing in a time like this," he said.

He served them warm cinnamon rolls just out of the oven, the icing still runny. He put butter on the table and knives to spread the butter. Then the baker sat down at the table with them. He waited. He waited until they each took a roll from the platter and began to eat. "It's good to eat something," he said, watching them. "There's more. Eat up. Eat all you want. There's all the rolls in the world in here."

They ate rolls and drank coffee. Ann was suddenly hungry, and the rolls were warm and sweet. She ate three of them, which pleased the baker. Then he began to talk. They listened carefully. Although they were tired and in anguish, they listened to what the baker had to say. They nodded when the baker began to speak of loneliness, and of the sense of doubt and limitation that had come to him in his middle years. He told them what it was like to be childless all these years. To repeat the days with the ovens endlessly full and endlessly empty. The party food, the celebrations he'd worked over. Icing knuckle-deep. The tiny wedding couples stuck into cakes. Hundreds of them, no, thousands by now. Birthdays. Just imagine all those candles burning. He had a necessary trade. He was a baker. He was glad he wasn't a florist. It was better to be feeding people. This was a better smell anytime than flowers.

"Smell this," the baker said, breaking open a dark loaf. "It's a heavy bread, but rich." They smelled it, then he had them taste it. It had the taste of molasses and coarse grains. They listened to him. They ate what they could. They swallowed the dark bread. It was like daylight under the fluorescent trays of light. They talked on into the early morning, the high, pale cast of light in the windows, and they did not think of leaving.

Vitamins

I had a job and Patti didn't. I worked a few hours a night for the hospital. It was a nothing job. I did some work, signed the card for eight hours, went drinking with the nurses. After a while, Patti wanted a job. She said she needed a job for her self-respect. So she started selling multiple vitamins door to door.

For a while, she was just another girl who went up and down blocks in strange neighborhoods, knocking on doors. But she learned the ropes. She was quick and had excelled at things in school. She had personality. Pretty soon the company gave her a promotion. Some of the girls who weren't doing so hot were put to work under her. Before long, she had herself a crew and a little office out in the mall. But the girls who worked for her were always changing. Some would quit after a couple of days – after a couple of hours, sometimes. But sometimes there were girls who were good at it. They could sell vitamins. These were the girls that stuck with Patti. They formed the core of the crew. But there were girls who couldn't give away vitamins.

The girls who couldn't cut it would just quit. Just not show up for work. If they had a phone, they'd take it off the hook. They wouldn't answer the door. Patti took these losses to heart, like the girls were new converts who had lost their way. She blamed herself. But she got over it. There were too many not to get over it.

Once in a while a girl would freeze and not be able to push the doorbell. Or maybe she'd get to the door and something would happen to her voice. Or she'd get the greeting mixed up with something she shouldn't be saying until she got inside. A girl like this, she'd decide to pack it in, take the sample case, head for the car, hang around until Patti and the others finished. There'd be a conference. Then they'd all ride back to the office. They'd say things to buck themselves up. "When the going gets tough, the tough get going." And, "Do the right things and the right things will happen." Things like that.

Sometimes a girl just disappeared in the field, sample case and all. She'd hitch a ride into town, then beat it. But there were always girls to take her place. Girls were coming and going in those days. Patti had a list. Every few weeks she'd run a little ad in *The Pennysaver*. There'd be more girls and more training. There was no end of girls.

The core group was made up of Patti, Donna, and Sheila. Patti was a looker. Donna and Sheila were only medium-pretty. One night this Sheila said to Patti that she loved her more than anything on earth. Patti told me these were the words. Patti had driven Sheila home and they were sitting in front of Sheila's place. Patti said to Sheila she loved her, too. Patti said to Sheila she loved all her girls. But not in the way Sheila had in mind. Then Sheila touched Patti's breast. Patti said she took Sheila's hand and held it. She said she told her she didn't swing that way. She said Sheila didn't bat an eye, that she only nodded, held on to Patti's hand, kissed it, and got out of the car.

That was around Christmas. The vitamin business was pretty bad off back then, so we thought we'd have a party to cheer everybody up. It seemed like a good idea at the time. Sheila was the first to get drunk and pass out. She passed out on her feet, fell over, and didn't wake up for hours. One minute she was standing in the middle of the living room, then her eyes closed, the legs buckled, and she went down with a glass in her hand. The hand holding the drink smacked the coffee table when she fell. She didn't make a sound otherwise. The drink poured out onto the rug. Patti and I and somebody else lugged her out to the back porch and put her down on a cot and did what we could to forget about her.

Everybody got drunk and went home. Patti went to bed. I wanted to keep on, so I sat at the table with a drink until it began to get light out. Then Sheila came in from the porch and started up. She said she had this headache that was so bad it was like somebody was sticking wires in her brain. She said it was such a bad headache she was afraid it was going to leave her with a permanent squint. And she was sure her little finger was broken. She showed it to me. It looked purple. She bitched about us letting her sleep all night with her contacts in. She wanted to know didn't anybody give a shit. She brought the finger up close and looked at it. She shook her head. She held the finger as far away as she could and looked some more. It was like she couldn't believe the things that must have happened to her that night. Her face was puffy, and her hair was all over. She ran cold water on her finger. "God. Oh, God," she said and cried some over the sink. But she'd made a serious pass at Patti, a declaration of love, and I didn't have any sympathy.

I was drinking Scotch and milk with a sliver of ice. Sheila was leaning on the drainboard. She watched me from her little slits of eyes. I took some of my drink. I didn't say anything. She went back to telling me how bad she felt. She said she needed to see a doctor. She said she was going to wake Patti. She said she was quitting, leaving the state, going to Portland. That she had to say goodbye to Patti first. She kept on. She wanted Patti to drive her to the hospital for her finger and her eyes.

"I'll drive you," I said. I didn't want to do it, but I would.

"I want Patti to drive me," Sheila said.

She was holding the wrist of her bad hand with her good hand, the little finger as big as a pocket flashlight. "Besides, we need to talk. I need to tell her I'm going to Portland. I need to say goodbye."

I said, "I guess I'll have to tell her for you. She's asleep."

Sheila turned mean. "We're friends," she said. "I have to talk to her. I have to tell her myself."

I shook my head. "She's asleep. I just said so."

"We're friends and we love each other," Sheila said. "I have to say goodbye to her."

Sheila made to leave the kitchen.

I started to get up. I said, "I said I'll drive you."

"You're drunk! You haven't even been to bed yet." She looked at her finger again and said, "Goddamn, why'd this have to happen?"

"Not too drunk to drive you to the hospital," I said.

"I won't ride with you!" Sheila yelled.

"Suit yourself. But you're not going to wake Patti. Lesbo bitch," I said.

"Bastard," she said.

That's what she said, and then she went out of the kitchen and out the front door without using the bathroom or even washing her face. I got up and looked through the window. She was walking down the road toward Euclid. Nobody else was up. It was too early.

I finished my drink and thought about fixing another one. I fixed it.

Nobody saw any more of Sheila after that. None of us vitamin-related people, anyway. She walked to Euclid Avenue and out of our lives.

Later on Patti said, "What happened to Sheila?" and I said, "She went to Portland."

I had the hots for Donna, the other member of the core group. We'd danced to some Duke Ellington records that night of the party. I'd held her pretty tight, smelled her hair, kept a hand low on her back as I moved her over the rug. It was great dancing with her. I was the only fellow at the party, and there were seven girls, six of them dancing with each other. It was great just looking around the living room.

I was in the kitchen when Donna came in with her empty glass. We were alone for a bit. I got her into a little embrace. She hugged me back. We stood there and hugged.

Then she said, "Don't. Not now."

When I heard that "Not now," I let go. I figured it was money in the bank.

I'd been at the table thinking about that hug when Sheila came in with her finger.

I thought some more about Donna. I finished the drink. I took the phone off the hook and headed for the bedroom. I took off my clothes and got in next to Patti. I lay for a while, winding down. Then I started in. But she didn't wake up. Afterwards, I closed my eyes.

It was the afternoon when I opened them again. I was in bed alone. Rain was blowing against the window. A sugar doughnut was lying on Patti's pillow, and a glass of old water was on the nightstand. I was still drunk and couldn't figure anything out. I knew it was Sunday and close to Christmas. I ate the doughnut and drank the water. I went back to sleep until I heard Patti running the vacuum. She came into the bedroom and asked about Sheila. That's when I told her, said she'd gone to Portland.

A week or so into the new year, Patti and I were having a drink. She'd just come home from work. It wasn't so late, but it was dark and rainy. I was going to work in a couple of hours. But first we were having us some Scotch and talking. Patti was tired. She was down in the dumps and into her third drink. Nobody was buying vitamins. All she had was Donna and Pam, a semi-new girl who was a klepto. We were talking about things like negative weather and the number of parking tickets you could get away with. Then we got to talking about how we'd be better off if we moved to Arizona, someplace like that.

I fixed us another one. I looked out the window. Arizona wasn't a bad idea.

Patti said, "Vitamins." She picked up her glass and spun the ice. "For shit's sake!" she said. "I mean, when I was a girl, this is the last thing I ever saw myself doing. Jesus, I never thought I'd grow up to sell vitamins. Door-to-door vitamins. This beats all. This really blows my mind."

"I never thought so either, honey," I said.

"That's right," she said. "You said it in a nutshell."

"Honey."

"Don't honey me," she said. "This is hard, brother. This life is not easy, any way you cut it."

She seemed to think things over for a bit. She shook her head. Then she finished her drink. She said, "I even dream of vitamins when I'm asleep. I don't have any relief. There's no relief ! At least you can walk away from your job and leave it behind. I'll bet you haven't had one dream about it. I'll bet you don't dream about waxing floors or whatever you do down there. After you've left the goddamn place, you don't come home and dream about it, do you?" she screamed.

I said, "I can't remember what I dream. Maybe I don't dream. I don't remember anything when I wake up." I shrugged. I didn't keep track of what went on in my head when I was asleep. I didn't care.

"You dream!" Patti said. "Even if you don't remember. Everybody dreams. If you didn't dream, you'd go crazy. I read about it. It's an outlet. People dream when they're asleep. Or else they'd go nuts. But when I dream, I dream of vitamins. Do you see what I'm saying?" She had her eyes fixed on me.

"Yes and no," I said.

It wasn't a simple question.

"I dream I'm pitching vitamins," she said. "I'm selling vitamins day and night. Jesus, what a life," she said.

She finished her drink.

"How's Pam doing?" I said. "She still stealing things?" I wanted to get us off this subject. But there wasn't anything else I could think of.

Patti said, "Shit," and shook her head like I didn't know anything. We listened to it rain.

"Nobody's selling vitamins," Patti said. She picked up her glass. But it was empty. "Nobody's buying vitamins. That's what I'm telling you. Didn't you hear me?"

I got up to fix us another. "Donna doing anything?" I said. I read the label on the bottle and waited.

Patti said, "She made a little sale two days ago. That's all. That's all that any of us has done this week. It wouldn't surprise me if she quit. I wouldn't blame her,' Patti said. "if I was in her place, I'd quit. But if she quits, then what? Then I'm back at the start, that's what. Ground zero. Middle of winter, people sick all over the state, people dying, and nobody thinks they need vitamins. I'm sick as hell myself."

"What's wrong, honey?" I put the drinks on the table and sat down. She went on like I hadn't said anything. Maybe I hadn't.

"I'm my only customer," she said. "I think taking all these vitamins is doing something to my skin. Does my skin look okay to you? Can a person get overdosed on vitamins? I'm getting to where I can't even take a crap like a normal person."

"Honey," I said.

Patti said, "You don't care if I take vitamins. That's the point. You don't care about anything. The windshield wiper quit this afternoon in the rain. I almost had a wreck. I came this close."

We went on drinking and talking until it was time for me to go to work. Patti said she was going to soak in a tub if she didn't fall asleep first. "I'm asleep on my feet," she said. She said, "Vitamins. That's all there is anymore." She looked around the kitchen. She looked at her empty glass. She was drunk. But she let me kiss her. Then I left for work.

There was a place I went to after work. I'd started going for the music and because I could get a drink there after closing hours. It was a place called the Off-Broadway. It was a spade place in a spade neighborhood. It was run by a spade named Khaki. People would show up after the other places had stopped serving. They'd ask for house specials – RC Colas with a shooter of whiskey – or else they'd bring in their own stuff under their coats, order RC, and build their own. Musicians showed up to jam, and the drinkers who wanted to keep drinking came to drink and listen to the music. Sometimes people danced. But mainly they sat around and drank and listened.

Now and then a spade hit a spade in the head with a

bottle. A story went around once that somebody had followed somebody into the Gents and cut the man's throat while he had his hands down pissing. But I never saw any trouble. Nothing that Khaki couldn't handle. Khaki was a big spade with a bald head that lit up weird under the fluorescents. He wore Hawaiian shirts that hung over his pants. I think he carried something inside his waistband. At least a sap, maybe. If somebody started to get out of line, Khaki would go over to where it was beginning. He'd rest his big hand on the party's shoulder and say a few words and that was that. I'd been going there off and on for months. I was pleased that he'd say things to me, things like, "How're you doing tonight, friend?" Or, "Friend, I haven't seen you for a spell."

The Off-Broadway is where I took Donna on our date. It was the one date we ever had.

I'd walked out of the hospital just after midnight. It'd cleared up and stars were out. I still had this buzz on from the Scotch I'd had with Patti. But I was thinking to hit New Jimmy's for a quick one on the way home. Donna's car was parked in the space next to my car, and Donna was inside the car. I remembered that hug we'd had in the kitchen. "Not now," she'd said.

She rolled the window down and knocked ashes from her cigarette.

"I couldn't sleep," she said. "I have some things on my mind, and I couldn't sleep."

I said, "Donna. Hey, I'm glad to see you, Donna."

"I don't know what's wrong with me," she said.

"You want to go someplace for a drink?" I said.

"Patti's my friend," she said.

"She's my friend, too," I said. Then I said, "Let's go."

"Just so you know," she said.

"There's this place. It's a spade place," I said. "They have music. We can get a drink, listen to some music."

"You want to drive me?" Donna said.

I said, "Scoot over."

She started right in about vitamins. Vitamins were on the skids, vitamins had taken a nosedive. The bottom had fallen out of the vitamin market.

Donna said, "I hate to do this to Patti. She's my best friend, and she's trying to build things up for us. But I may have to quit. This is between us. Swear it! But I have to eat. I have to pay rent. I need new shoes and a new coat. Vitamins can't cut it," Donna said. "I don't think vitamins is where it's at anymore. I haven't said anything to Patti. Like I said, I'm still just thinking about it."

Donna laid her hand next to my leg. I reached down and squeezed her fingers. She squeezed back. Then she took her hand away and pushed in the lighter. After she had her cigarette going, she put the hand back. "Worse than anything, I hate to let Patti down. You know what I'm saying? We were a team." She reached me her cigarette. "I know it's a different brand," she said, "but try it, go ahead."

I pulled into the lot for the Off-Broadway. Three spades were up against an old Chrysler that had a cracked windshield. They were just lounging, passing a bottle in a sack. They looked us over. I got out and went around to open up for Donna. I checked the doors, took her arm, and we headed for the street. The spades just watched us.

I said, "You're not thinking about moving to Portland, are you?"

We were on the sidewalk. I put my arm around her waist.

"I don't know anything about Portland. Portland hasn't crossed my mind once."

The front half of the Off-Broadway was like a regular café and bar. A few spades sat at the counter and a few more worked over plates of food at tables with red oilcloth. We went through the café and into the big room in back. There was a long counter with booths against the wall and farther back a platform where musicians could set up. In front of the platform was what passed for a dance floor. The bars and nightclubs were still serving, so people hadn't turned up in any real numbers yet. I helped Donna take off her coat. We picked a booth and put our cigarettes on the table. The spade waitress named Hannah came over. Hannah and me nodded. She looked at Donna. I ordered us two RC specials and decided to feel good about things.

After the drinks came and I'd paid and we'd each had a sip, we started hugging. We carried on like this for a while, squeezing and patting, kissing each other's face. Every so often Donna would stop and draw back, push me away a little, then hold me by the wrists. She'd gaze into my eyes. Then her lids would close slowly and we'd fall to kissing again. Pretty soon the place began to fill up. We stopped kissing. But I kept my arm around her. She put her fingers on my leg. A couple of spade horn-players and a white drummer began fooling around with something. I figured Donna and me would have another drink and listen to the set. Then we'd leave and go to her place to finish things.

I'd just ordered two more from Hannah when this spade named Benny came over with this other spade – this big, dressed-up spade. This big spade had little red eyes and was wearing a three-piece pinstripe. He had on a rose-colored shirt, a tie, a topcoat, a fedora – all of it.

'How's my man?" said Benny.

Benny stuck out his hand for a brother handshake. Benny and I had talked. He knew I liked the music, and he used to come over to talk whenever we were both in the place. He liked to talk about Johnny Hodges, how he'd played sax backup for Johnny. He'd say things like, "When Johnny and me had this gig in Mason City."

"Hi, Benny," I said.

"I want you to meet Nelson," Benny said. "He just back from Nam today. This morning. He here to listen to some of these good sounds. He got on his dancing shoes in case." Benny looked at Nelson and nodded. "This here is Nelson."

I was looking at Nelson's shiny shoes, and then I looked at Nelson. He seemed to want to place me from somewhere. He studied me. Then he let loose a rolling grin that showed his teeth.

"This is Donna," I said. "Donna, this is Benny, and this is Nelson. Nelson, this is Donna."

"Hello, girl," Nelson said, and Donna said right back, "Hello there, Nelson. Hello, Benny."

"Maybe we'll just slide in and join you folks?" Benny said. "Okay?"

I said, "Sure."

But I was sorry they hadn't found someplace else.

"We're not going to be here long," I said. "Just long enough to finish this drink, is all."

"I know, man, I know," Benny said. He sat across from me after Nelson had let himself down into the booth. "Things to do, places to go. Yes sir, Benny knows," Benny said, and winked.

Nelson looked across the booth to Donna. Then he took off the hat. He seemed to be looking for something on the brim as he turned the hat around in his big hands. He made room for the hat on the table. He looked up at Donna. He grinned and squared his shoulders. He had to square his

shoulders every few minutes. It was like he was very tired of
carrying them around.

"You real good friends with him, I bet," Nelson said to
Donna.

"We're good friends," Donna said.

Hannah came over. Benny asked for RCs. Hannah went
away, and Nelson worked a pint of whiskey from his topcoat.

"Good friends," Nelson said. "Real good friends." He
unscrewed the cap on his whiskey.

"Watch it, Nelson," Benny said. "Keep that out of sight.
Nelson just got off the plane from Nam," Benny said.

Nelson raised the bottle and drank some of his whiskey.
He screwed the cap back on, laid the bottle on the table, and
put his hat down on top of it. "Real good friends," he said.

Benny looked at me and rolled his eyes. But he was drunk,
too. "I got to get into shape," he said to me. He drank RC
from both of their glasses and then held the glasses under the
table and poured whiskey. He put the bottle in his coat
pocket. "Man, I ain't put my lips to a reed for a month now.
I got to get with it."

We were bunched in the booth, glasses in front of us,
Nelson's hat on the table. "You," Nelson said to me. "You
with somebody else, ain't you? This beautiful woman, she
ain't your wife. I know that. But you real good friends with
this woman. Ain't I right?"

I had some of my drink. I couldn't taste the whiskey.
I couldn't taste anything. I said, "Is all that shit about Vietnam
true we see on the TV?"

Nelson had his red eyes fixed on me. He said, "What I want
to say is, do you know where your wife is? I bet she out
with some dude and she be seizing his nipples for him and
pulling his pud for him while you setting here big as life with
your good friend. I bet she have herself a good friend, too."

"Nelson," Benny said.

"Nelson nothing," Nelson said.

Benny said, "Nelson, let's leave these people be. There's somebody in that other booth. Somebody I told you about. Nelson just this morning got off a plane," Benny said.

"I bet I know what you thinking," Nelson said. "I bet you thinking, 'Now here a big drunk nigger and what am I going to do with him? Maybe I have to whip his ass for him!' That what you thinking?"

I looked around the room. I saw Khaki standing near the platform, the musicians working away behind him. Some dancers were on the floor. I thought Khaki looked right at me – but if he did, he looked away again.

"Ain't it your turn to talk?" Nelson said. "I just teasing you. I ain't done any teasing since I left Nam. I teased the gooks some." He grinned again, his big lips rolling back. Then he stopped grinning and just stared.

"Show them that ear," Benny said. He put his glass on the table. "Nelson got himself an ear off one of them little dudes," Benny said. "He carry it with him. Show them, Nelson."

Nelson sat there. Then he started feeling the pockets of his topcoat. He took things out of one pocket. He took out some keys and a box of cough drops.

Donna said, "I don't want to see an ear. Ugh. Double ugh. Jesus." She looked at me.

"We have to go," I said.

Nelson was still feeling in his pockets. He took a wallet from a pocket inside the suit coat and put it on the table. He patted the wallet. "Five big ones there. Listen here," he said to Donna. "I going to give you two bills. You with me? I give you two big ones, and then you French me. Just like his woman doing some other big fellow. You hear? You know she got her mouth on somebody's hammer right this minute while he here with his hand up your skirt. Fair's fair. Here." He pulled the corners of the bills from his wallet. "Hell, here another hundred for your good friend, so he won't feel left out. He don't have to do nothing. You don't have to do nothing," Nelson said to me. "You just sit there and drink your drink and listen to the music. Good music. Me and this woman walk out together like good friends. And she walk back in by herself. Won't be long, she be back."

"Nelson," Benny said, "this is no way to talk, Nelson."

Nelson grinned. "I finished talking," he said.

He found what he'd been feeling for. It was a silver cigarette case. He opened it up. I looked at the ear inside. It sat on a bed of cotton. It looked like a dried mushroom. But it was a real ear, and it was hooked up to a key chain.

"Jesus," said Donna. "Yuck."

"Ain't that something?" Nelson said. He was watching Donna.

"No way. Fuck off," Donna said.

"Girl," Nelson said.

"Nelson," I said. And then Nelson fixed his red eyes on me. He pushed the hat and wallet and cigarette case out of his way.

"What do you want?" Nelson said. "I give you what you want."

Khaki had a hand on my shoulder and the other one on Benny's shoulder. He leaned over the table, his head shining under the lights. "How you folks? You all having fun?"

"Everything all right, Khaki," Benny said. "Everything A-okay. These people here was just fixing to leave. Me and Nelson going to sit and listen to the music."

"That's good," Khaki said. "Folks be happy is my motto."

He looked around the booth. He looked at Nelson's wallet on the table and at the open cigarette case next to the wallet. He saw the ear.

"That a real ear?" Khaki said.

Benny said, "It is. Show him that ear, Nelson. Nelson just stepped off the plane from Nam with this ear. This ear has traveled halfway around the world to be on this table tonight. Nelson, show him," Benny said.

Nelson picked up the case and handed it to Khaki.

Khaki examined the ear. He took up the chain and dangled the ear in front of his face. He looked at it. He let it swing back and forth on the chain. "I heard about these dried-up ears and dicks and such."

"I took it off one of them gooks," Nelson said. "He couldn't hear nothing with it no more. I wanted me a keepsake."

Khaki turned the ear on its chain.

Donna and I began getting out of the booth.

"Girl, don't go," Nelson said.

"Nelson," Benny said.

Khaki was watching Nelson now. I stood beside the booth with Donna's coat. My legs were crazy.

Nelson raised his voice. He said, "You go with this mother here, you let him put his face in your sweets, you both going to have to deal with me."

We started to move away from the booth. People were looking.

"Nelson just got off the plane from Nam this morning," I heard Benny say. "We been drinking all day. This been the longest day on record. But me and him, we going to be fine, Khaki."

Nelson yelled something over the music. He yelled, "It ain't going to do no good! Whatever you do, it ain't going to help none!" I heard him say that, and then I couldn't hear anymore. The music stopped, and then it started again. We didn't look back. We kept going. We got out to the sidewalk.

I opened the door for her. I started us back to the hospital. Donna stayed over on her side. She'd used the lighter on a cigarette, but she wouldn't talk.

I tried to say something. I said, "Look, Donna, don't get on a downer because of this. I'm sorry it happened," I said.

"I could of used the money," Donna said. "That's what I was thinking."

I kept driving and didn't look at her.

"It's true," she said. "I could of used the money." She shook her head. "I don't know," she said. She put her chin down and cried.

"Don't cry," I said.

"I'm not going in to work tomorrow, today, whenever it is the alarm goes off," she said. "I'm not going in. I'm leaving town. I take what happened back there as a sign." She pushed in the lighter and waited for it to pop out.

I pulled in beside my car and killed the engine. I looked in the rearview, half thinking I'd see that old Chrysler drive into the lot behind me with Nelson in the seat. I kept my hands on the wheel for a minute, and then dropped them to my lap. I didn't want to touch Donna. The hug we'd given each other in my kitchen that night, the kissing we'd done at the Off-Broadway, that was all over.

I said, "What are you going to do?" But I didn't care. Right then she could have died of a heart attack and it wouldn't have meant anything.

"Maybe I could go up to Portland," she said. "There must be something in Portland. Portland's on everybody's mind these days. Portland's a drawing card. Portland this, Portland that. Portland's as good a place as any. It's all the same."

"Donna," I said, "I'd better go."

I started to let myself out. I cracked the door, and the overhead light came on.

"For Christ's sake, turn off that light!"

I got out in a hurry. "'Night, Donna," I said.

I left her staring at the dashboard. I started up my car and turned on the lights. I slipped it in gear and fed it the gas.

I poured Scotch, drank some of it, and took the glass into the bathroom. I brushed my teeth. Then I pulled open a drawer. Patti yelled something from the bedroom. She opened the bathroom door. She was still dressed. She'd been sleeping with her clothes on, I guess.

"What time is it?" she screamed. "I've overslept! Jesus, oh my God! You've let me oversleep, goddamn you!"

She was wild. She stood in the doorway with her clothes on. She could have been fixing to go to work. But there was no sample case, no vitamins. She was having a bad dream, is all. She began shaking her head from side to side.

I couldn't take any more tonight. "Go back to sleep, honey. I'm looking for something," I said. I knocked some stuff out of the medicine chest. Things rolled into the sink. "Where's the aspirin?" I said. I knocked down some more things. I didn't care. Things kept falling.

Careful

After a lot of talking – what his wife, Inez, called *assessment* –
Lloyd moved out of the house and into his own place. He
had two rooms and a bath on the top floor of a three-story
house. Inside the rooms, the roof slanted down sharply. If he
walked around, he had to duck his head. He had to stoop to
look from his windows and be careful getting in and out of
bed. There were two keys. One key let him into the house
itself. Then he climbed some stairs that passed through the
house to a landing. He went up another flight of stairs to
the door of his room and used the other key on that lock.

Once, when he was coming back to his place in the afternoon, carrying a sack with three bottles of André champagne
and some lunch meat, he stopped on the landing and looked
into his landlady's living room. He saw the old woman lying
on her back on the carpet. She seemed to be asleep. Then it
occurred to him she might be dead. But the TV was going,
so he chose to think she was asleep. He didn't know what to
make of it. He moved the sack from one arm to the other.
It was then that the woman gave a little cough, brought her
hand to her side, and went back to being quiet and still again.
Lloyd continued on up the stairs and unlocked his door.
Later that day, toward evening, as he looked from his kitchen
window, he saw the old woman down in the yard, wearing
a straw hat and holding her hand against her side. She was
using a little watering can on some pansies.

In his kitchen, he had a combination refrigerator and stove. The refrigerator and stove was a tiny affair wedged into a space between the sink and the wall. He had to bend over, almost get down on his knees, to get anything out of the refrigerator. But it was all right because he didn't keep much in there, anyway – except fruit juice, lunch meat, and champagne. The stove had two burners. Now and then he heated water in a saucepan and made instant coffee. But some days he didn't drink any coffee. He forgot, or else he just didn't feel like coffee. One morning he woke up and promptly fell to eating crumb doughnuts and drinking champagne. There'd been a time, some years back, when he would have laughed at having a breakfast like this. Now, there didn't seem to be anything very unusual about it. In fact, he hadn't thought anything about it until he was in bed and trying to recall the things he'd done that day, starting with when he'd gotten up that morning. At first, he couldn't remember anything noteworthy. Then he remembered eating those doughnuts and drinking champagne. Time was when he would have considered this a mildly crazy thing to do, something to tell friends about. Then, the more he thought about it, the more he could see it didn't matter much one way or the other. He'd had doughnuts and champagne for breakfast. So what?

In his furnished rooms, he also had a dinette set, a little sofa, an old easy chair, and a TV set that stood on a coffee table. He wasn't paying the electricity here, it wasn't even his TV, so sometimes he left the set on all day and all night. But he kept the volume down unless he saw there was something he wanted to watch. He did not have a telephone, which was fine with him. He didn't want a telephone. There was a bedroom with a double bed, a nightstand, a chest of drawers, a bathroom.

The one time Inez came to visit, it was eleven o'clock in the morning. He'd been in his new place for two weeks, and he'd been wondering if she were going to drop by. But he was trying to do something about his drinking, too, so he was glad to be alone. He'd made that much clear — being alone was the thing he needed most. The day she came, he was on the sofa, in his pyjamas, hitting his fist against the right side of his head. Just before he could hit himself again, he heard voices downstairs on the landing. He could make out his wife's voice. The sound was like the murmur of voices from a faraway crowd, but he knew it was Inez and somehow knew the visit was an important one. He gave his head another jolt with his fist, then got to his feet.

He'd awakened that morning and found that his ear had stopped up with wax. He couldn't hear anything clearly, and he seemed to have lost his sense of balance, his equilibrium, in the process. For the last hour, he'd been on the sofa, working frustratedly on his ear, now and again slamming his head with his fist. Once in a while he'd massage the gristly underpart of his ear, or else tug at his lobe. Then he'd dig furiously in his ear with his little finger and open his mouth, simulating yawns. But he'd tried everything he could think of, and he was nearing the end of his rope. He could hear the voices below break off their murmuring. He pounded his head a good one and finished the glass of champagne. He turned off the TV and carried the glass to the sink. He picked up the open bottle of champagne from the drain-board and took it into the bathroom, where he put it behind the stool. Then he went to answer the door.

"Hi, Lloyd," Inez said. She didn't smile. She stood in the doorway in a bright spring outfit. He hadn't seen these clothes before. She was holding a canvas handbag that had sunflowers stitched onto its sides. He hadn't seen the handbag before, either.

"I didn't think you heard me," she said. "I thought you might be gone or something. But the woman downstairs — what's her name? Mrs Matthews — she thought you were up here."

"I heard you," Lloyd said. "But just barely." He hitched his pyjamas and ran a hand through his hair. "Actually, I'm in one hell of a shape. Come on in."

"It's eleven o'clock," she said. She came inside and shut the door behind her. She acted as if she hadn't heard him. Maybe she hadn't.

"I know what time it is," he said. "I've been up for a long time. I've been up since eight. I watched part of the *Today* show. But just now I'm about to go crazy with something. My ear's plugged up. You remember that other time it happened? We were living in that place near the Chinese takeout joint. Where the kids found that bulldog dragging its chain? I had to go to the doctor then and have my ears flushed out. I know you remember. You drove me and we had to wait a long time. Well, it's like that now. I mean it's that bad. Only I can't go to a doctor this morning. I don't have a doctor for one thing. I'm about to go nuts, Inez. I feel like I want to cut my head off or something."

He sat down at one end of the sofa, and she sat down at the other end. But it was a small sofa, and they were still sitting close to each other. They were so close he could have put out his hand and touched her knee. But he didn't. She glanced around the room and then fixed her eyes on him again. He knew he hadn't shaved and that his hair stood up. But she was his wife, and she knew everything there was to know about him.

"What have you tried?" she said. She looked in her purse

and brought up a cigarette. "I mean, what have you done for it so far?"

"What'd you say?" He turned the left side of his head to her. "Inez, I swear, I'm not exaggerating. This thing is driving me crazy. When I talk, I feel like I'm talking inside a barrel. My head rumbles. And I can't hear good, either. When you talk, it sounds like you're talking through a lead pipe."

"Do you have any Q-tips, or else Wesson oil?" Inez said.

"Honey, this is serious," he said. "I don't have any Q-tips or Wesson oil. Are you kidding?"

"If we had some Wesson oil, I could heat it and put some of that in your ear. My mother used to do that," she said. "It might soften things up in there."

He shook his head. His head felt full and like it was awash with fluid. It felt like it had when he used to swim near the bottom of the municipal pool and come up with his ears filled with water. But back then it'd been easy to clear the water out. All he had to do was fill his lungs with air, close his mouth, and clamp down on his nose. Then he'd blow out his cheeks and force air into his head. His ears would pop, and for a few seconds he'd have the pleasant sensation of water running out of his head and dripping onto his shoulders. Then he'd heave himself out of the pool.

Inez finished her cigarette and put it out. "Lloyd, we have things to talk about. But I guess we'll have to take things one at a time. Go sit in the chair. Not *that* chair, the chair in the kitchen! So we can have some light on the situation."

He whacked his head once more. Then he went over to sit on a dinette chair. She moved over and stood behind him. She touched his hair with her fingers. Then she moved the hair away from his ears. He reached for her hand, but she drew it away.

"Which ear did you say it was?" she said.

"The right ear," he said. "The right one."

"First," she said, "you have to sit here and not move. I'll find a hairpin and some tissue paper. I'll try to get in there with that. Maybe it'll do the trick."

He was alarmed at the prospect of her putting a hairpin inside his ear. He said something to that effect.

"What?" she said. "Christ, I can't hear you, either. Maybe this is catching."

"When I was a kid, in school," Lloyd said, "we had this health teacher. She was like a nurse, too. She said we should never put anything smaller than an elbow into our ear." He vaguely remembered a wall chart showing a massive diagram of the ear, along with an intricate system of canals, passage-ways, and walls.

"Well, your nurse was never faced with this exact problem," Inez said. "Anyway, we need to try *something*. We'll try this first. If it doesn't work we'll try something else. That's life, isn't it?"

"Does that have a hidden meaning or something?" Lloyd said.

"It means just what I said. But you're free to think as you please. I mean, it's a free country," she said. "Now, let me get fixed up with what I need. You just sit there."

She went through her purse, but she didn't find what she was looking for. Finally, she emptied the purse out onto the sofa. "No hairpins," she said. "Damn." But it was as if she were saying the words from another room. In a way, it was almost as if he'd imagined her saying them. There'd been a time, long ago, when they used to feel they had ESP when it came to what the other one was thinking. They could finish sentences that the other had started.

She picked up some nail clippers, worked for a minute, and then he saw the device separate in her fingers and part of it swing away from the other part. A nail file protruded from the clippers. It looked to him as if she were holding a small dagger.

"You're going to put that in my ear?" he said.

"Maybe you have a better idea," she said. "It's this, or else I don't know what. Maybe you have a pencil? You want me to use that? Or maybe you have a screwdriver around," she said and laughed. "Don't worry. Listen, Lloyd, I won't hurt you. I said I'd be careful. I'll wrap some tissue around the end of this. It'll be all right. I'll be careful, like I said. You just stay where you are, and I'll get some tissue for this. I'll make a swab."

She went into the bathroom. She was gone for a time. He stayed where he was on the dinette chair. He began think-ing of things he ought to say to her. He wanted to tell her he was limiting himself to champagne and champagne only. He wanted to tell her he was tapering off the champagne, too. It was only a matter of time now. But when she came back into the room, he couldn't say anything. He didn't know where to start. But she didn't look at him, anyway. She fished a cigarette from the heap of things she'd emptied onto the sofa cushion. She lit the cigarette with her lighter and went to stand by the window that faced onto the street. She said something, but he couldn't make out the words. When she stopped talking, he didn't ask her what it was she'd said. Whatever it was, he knew he didn't want her to say it again. She put out the cigarette. But she went on standing at the window, leaning forward, the slope of the roof just inches from her head.

"Inez," he said.

She turned and came over to him. He could see tissue on the point of the nail file.

"Turn your head to the side and keep it that way," she said.

"That's right. Sit still now and don't move. Don't move," she said again.

"Be careful," he said. "For Christ's sake."

She didn't answer him.

"Please, please," he said. Then he didn't say any more. He was afraid. He closed his eyes and held his breath as he felt the nail file turn past the inner part of his ear and begin its probe. He was sure his heart would stop beating. Then she went a little farther and began turning the blade back and forth, working at whatever it was in there. Inside his ear, he heard a squeaking sound.

"Ouch!" he said.

"Did I hurt you?" She took the nail file out of his ear and moved back a step. "Does anything feel different, Lloyd?"

He brought his hands up to his ears and lowered his head.

"It's just the same," he said.

She looked at him and bit her lips.

"Let me go to the bathroom," he said. "Before we go any farther, I have to go to the bathroom."

"Go ahead," Inez said. "I think I'll go downstairs and see if your landlady has any Wesson oil, or anything like that. She might even have some Q-tips. I don't know why I didn't think of that before. Of asking her."

"That's a good idea," he said. "I'll go to the bathroom."

She stopped at the door and looked at him, and then she opened the door and went out. He crossed the living room, went into his bedroom, and opened the bathroom door. He reached down behind the stool and brought up the bottle of champagne. He took a long drink. It was warm but it went right down. He took some more. In the beginning, he'd really thought he could continue drinking if he limited himself to champagne. But in no time he found he was drinking three or four bottles a day. He knew he'd have to deal with this pretty soon. But first, he'd have to get his hearing back. One thing at a time, just like she'd said. He finished off the rest of the champagne and put the empty bottle in its place behind the stool. Then he ran water and brushed his teeth. After he'd used the towel, he went back into the other room.

Inez had returned and was at the stove heating something in a little pan. She glanced in his direction, but didn't say anything at first. He looked past her shoulder and out the window. A bird flew from one tree to another and preened its feathers. But if it made any kind of bird noise, he didn't hear it.

She said something that he didn't catch.

"Say again," he said.

She shook her head and turned back to the stove. But then she turned again and said, loud enough and slow enough so he could hear it: "I found your stash in the bathroom."

"I'm trying to cut back," he said.

She said something else. "What?" he said. "What'd you say?" He really hadn't heard her.

"We'll talk later," she said. "We have things to discuss, Lloyd. Money is one thing. But there are other things, too. First we have to see about this ear." She put her finger into the pan and then took the pan off the stove. "I'll let it cool for a minute," she said. "It's too hot right now. Sit down. Put this towel around your shoulders."

He did as he was told. He sat on a chair and put the towel around his neck and shoulders. Then he hit the side of his head with his fist.

"Goddamn it," he said.

She didn't look up. She put her finger into the pan once more, testing. Then she poured the liquid from the pan into his plastic glass. She picked up the glass and came over to him.

"Don't be scared, " she said. "it's just some of your land-lady's baby oil, that's all it is. I told her what was wrong, and she thought this might help. No guarantees," Inez said. "But maybe this'll loosen things up in there. She said it used to happen to her husband. She said this one time she saw a piece of wax fall out of his ear, and it was like a big plug of something. It was ear wax, was what it was. She said try this. And she didn't have any Q-tips. I can't understand that, her not having any Q-tips. That part really surprises me."

"Okay," he said. "All right. I'm willing to try anything. Inez, if I had to go on like this, I think I'd rather be dead. You know? I mean it, Inez."

"Tilt your head all the way to the side now," she said. "Don't move. I'll pour this in until your ear fills up, then I'll stopper it with this dishrag. And you just sit there for ten minutes, say. Then we'll see. If this doesn't do it, well, I don't have any other suggestions. I just don't know what to do then."

"This'll work," he said. "If this doesn't work, I'll find a gun and shoot myself. I'm serious. That's what I feel like doing, anyway."

He turned his head to the side and let it hang down. He looked at the things in the room from this new perspective. But it wasn't any different from the old way of looking, except that everything was on its side.

"Farther," she said. He held on to the chair for balance and lowered his head even more. All of the objects in his vision, all of the objects in his life, it seemed, were at the far end of this room. He could feel the warm liquid pour into his ear. Then she brought the dishrag up and held it there. In a little while, she began to massage the area around his ear. She pressed into the soft part of the flesh between his jaw and skull. She moved her fingers to the area over his ear and began to work the tips of her fingers back and forth. After a while, he didn't know how long he'd been sitting there. It could have been ten minutes. It could have been longer. He was still holding on to the chair. Now and then, as her fingers pressed the side of his head, he could feel the warm oil she'd poured in there wash back and forth in the canals inside his ear. When she pressed a certain way, he imagined he could hear, inside his head, a soft, swishing sound.

"Sit up straight," Inez said. He sat up and pressed the heel of his hand against his head while the liquid poured out of his ear. She caught it in the towel. Then she wiped the outside of his ear.

Inez was breathing through her nose. Lloyd heard the sound her breath made as it came and went. He heard a car pass on the street outside the house and, at the back of the house, down below his kitchen window, the clear *snick-snick* of pruning shears. "Well?" Inez said. She waited with her hands on her hips, frowning.

"I can hear you," he said. "I'm all right! I mean, I can *hear*. It doesn't sound like you're talking underwater anymore. It's fine now. It's okay. God, I thought for a while I was going to go crazy. But I feel fine now. I can hear everything. Listen, honey, I'll make coffee. There's some juice, too."

"I have to go," she said. "I'm late for something. But I'll come back. We'll go out for lunch sometime. We need to talk."

"I just can't sleep on this side of my head, is all," he went on. He followed her into the living room. She lit a cigarette. "That's what happened. I slept all night on this side of my head, and my ear plugged up. I think I'll be all right as long as I don't forget and sleep on this side of my head. If I'm careful. You know what I'm saying? If I can just sleep on my back, or else on my left side."

She didn't look at him.

"Not forever, of course not, I know that. I couldn't do that. I couldn't do it the rest of my life. But for a while, anyway. Just my left side, or else flat on my back."

But even as he said this, he began to feel afraid of the night that was coming. He began to fear the moment he would begin to make his preparations for bed and what might happen afterward. That time was hours away, but already he was afraid. What if, in the middle of the night, he accidentally turned onto his right side, and the weight of his head pressing into the pillow were to seal the wax again into the dark canals of his ear? What if he woke up then, unable to hear, the ceiling inches from his head?

"Good God," he said. "Jesus, this is awful. Inez, I just had something like a terrible nightmare. Inez, where do you have to go?"

"I told you," she said, as she put everything back into her purse and made ready to leave. She looked at her watch. "I'm late for something." She went to the door. But at the door she turned and said something else to him. He didn't listen. He didn't want to. He watched her lips move until she'd said what she had to say. When she'd finished, she said, "Goodbye." Then she opened the door and closed it behind her.

He went into the bedroom to dress. But in a minute he hurried out, wearing only his trousers, and went to the door. He opened it and stood there, listening. On the landing below, he heard Inez thank Mrs Matthews for the oil. He heard the old woman say, "You're welcome." And then he heard her draw a connection between her late husband and himself. He heard her say, "Leave me your number. I'll call if something happens. You never know."

"I hope you don't have to," Inez said. "But I'll give it to

you, anyway. Do you have something to write it down with?"

Lloyd heard Mrs Matthews open a drawer and rummage through it. Then her old woman's voice said, "Okay."

Inez gave her their telephone number at home. "Thanks," she said.

"It was nice meeting you," Mrs Matthews said.

He listened as Inez went on down the stairs and opened the front door. Then he heard it close. He waited until he heard her start their car and drive away. Then he shut the door and went back into the bedroom to finish dressing.

After he'd put on his shoes and tied the laces, he lay down on the bed and pulled the covers up to his chin. He let his arms rest under the covers at his sides. He closed his eyes and pretended it was night and pretended he was going to fall asleep. Then he brought his arms up and crossed them over his chest to see how this position would suit him. He kept his eyes closed, trying it out. All right, he thought. Okay. If he didn't want that ear to plug up again, he'd have to sleep on his back, that was all. He knew he could do it. He just couldn't forget, even in his sleep, and turn onto the wrong side. Four or five hours' sleep a night was all he needed, anyway. He'd manage. Worse things could happen to a man. In a way, it was a challenge. But he was up to it. He knew he was. In a minute, he threw back the covers and got up.

He still had the better part of the day ahead of him. He went into the kitchen, bent down in front of the little refrigerator, and took out a fresh bottle of champagne. He worked the plastic cork out of the bottle as carefully as he could, but there was still the festive pop of champagne being opened. He rinsed the baby oil out of his glass, then poured it full of champagne. He took the glass over to the sofa and sat down. He put the glass on the coffee table. Up went his feet onto the coffee table, next to the champagne. He leaned back. But after a time he began to worry some more about the night· that was coming on. What if, despite all his efforts, the wax decided to plug his other ear? He closed his eyes and shook his head. Pretty soon he got up and went into the bedroom. He undressed and put his pyjamas back on. Then he moved back into the living room. He sat down on the sofa once more, and once more put his feet up. He reached over and turned the TV on. He adjusted the volume. He knew he couldn't keep from worrying about what might happen when he went to bed. It was just something he'd have to learn to live with. In a way, this whole business reminded him of the thing with the doughnuts and champagne. It was not that remarkable at all, if you thought about it. He took some champagne. But it didn't taste right. He ran his tongue over his lips, then wiped his mouth on his sleeve. He looked and saw a film of oil on the champagne.

He got up and carried the glass to the sink, where he poured it into the drain. He took the bottle of champagne into the living room and made himself comfortable on the sofa. He held the bottle by its neck as he drank. He wasn't in the habit of drinking from the bottle, but it didn't seem that much out of the ordinary. He decided that even if he were to fall asleep sitting up on the sofa in the middle of the afternoon, it wouldn't be any more strange than somebody having to lie on his back for hours at a time. He lowered his head to peer out the window. Judging from the angle of sunlight, and the shadows that had entered the room, he guessed it was about three o'clock.

Where I'm Calling From

J.P. and I are on the front porch at Frank Martin's drying-out facility. Like the rest of us at Frank Martin's, J.P. is first and foremost a drunk. But he's also a chimney sweep. It's his first time here, and he's scared. I've been here once before. What's to say? I'm back. J.P.'s real name is Joe Penny, but he says I should call him J. P. He's about thirty years old. Younger than I am. Not much younger, but a little. He's telling me how he decided to go into his line of work, and he wants to use his hands when he talks. But his hands tremble. I mean, they won't keep still. "This has never happened to me before," he says. He means the trembling. I tell him I sympathize. I tell him the shakes will idle down. And they will. But it takes time.

We've only been in here a couple of days. We're not out of the woods yet. J.P. has these shakes, and every so often a nerve – maybe it isn't a nerve, but it's something – begins to jerk in my shoulder. Sometimes it's at the side of my neck. When this happens, my mouth dries up. It's an effort just to swallow then. I know something's about to happen and I want to head it off. I want to hide from it, that's what I want to do. Just close my eyes and let it pass by, let it take the next man. J.P. can wait a minute.

I saw a seizure yesterday morning. A guy they call Tiny. A big fat guy, an electrician from Santa Rosa. They said he'd been in here for nearly two weeks and that he was over the hump. He was going home in a day or two and would spend New Year's Eve with his wife in front of the TV. On New Year's Eve, Tiny planned to drink hot chocolate and eat cookies. Yesterday morning he seemed just fine when he came down for breakfast. He was letting out with quacking noises, showing some guy how he called ducks right down onto his head. "Blam. Blam," said Tiny, picking off a couple. Tiny's hair was damp and was slicked back along the sides of his head. He'd just come out of the shower. He'd also nicked himself on the chin with his razor. But so what? Just about everybody at Frank Martin's has nicks on his face. It's something that happens. Tiny edged in at the head of the table and began telling about something that had happened on one of his drinking bouts. People at the table laughed and shook their heads as they shoveled up their eggs. Tiny would say something, grin, then look around the table for a sign of recognition. We'd all done things just as bad and crazy, so, sure, that's why we laughed. Tiny had scrambled eggs on his plate, and some biscuits and honey. I was at the table, but I wasn't hungry. I had some coffee in front of me. Suddenly, Tiny wasn't there anymore. He'd gone over in his chair with a big clatter. He was on his back on the floor with his eyes closed, his heels drumming the linoleum. People hollered for Frank Martin. But he was right there. A couple of guys got down on the floor beside Tiny. One of the guys put his fingers inside Tiny's mouth and tried to hold his tongue. Frank Martin yelled, "Everybody stand back!" Then I noticed that the bunch of us were leaning over Tiny, just looking at him, not able to take our eyes off him. "Give him air!" Frank Martin said. Then he ran into the office and called the ambulance.

Tiny is on board again today. Talk about bouncing back. This morning Frank Martin drove the station wagon to the hospital to get him. Tiny got back too late for his eggs, but he took some coffee into the dining room and sat down at the table anyway. Somebody in the kitchen made toast for him, but Tiny didn't eat it. He just sat with his coffee and looked into his cup. Every now and then he moved his cup back and forth in front of him.

I'd like to ask him if he had any signal just before it happened. I'd like to know if he felt his ticker skip a beat, or else begin to race. Did his eyelid twitch? But I'm not about to say anything. He doesn't look like he's hot to talk about it, anyway. But what happened to Tiny is something I won't ever forget. Old Tiny flat on the floor, kicking his heels. So every time this little flitter starts up anywhere, I draw some breath and wait to find myself on my back, looking up, somebody's fingers in my mouth.

In his chair on the front porch, J.P. keeps his hands in his lap. I smoke cigarettes and use an old coal bucket for an ashtray. I listen to J.P. ramble on. It's eleven o'clock in the morning – an hour and a half until lunch. Neither one of us is hungry. But just the same we look forward to going inside and sitting down at the table. Maybe we'll get hungry.

What's J.P. talking about, anyway? He's saying how when he was twelve years old he fell into a well in the vicinity of the farm he grew up on. It was a dry well, lucky for him. "Or unlucky," he says, looking around him and shaking his head. He says how late that afternoon, after he'd been located, his dad hauled him out with a rope. J.P. had wet his pants down there. He'd suffered all kinds of terror in that well, hollering for help, waiting, and then hollering some more. He hollered himself hoarse before it was over. But he told me that being at the bottom of that well had made a lasting impression. He'd sat there and looked up at the well mouth. Way up at the top, he could see a circle of blue sky. Every once in a while a white cloud passed over. A flock of birds flew across, and it seemed to J.P. their wingbeats set up this odd commotion. He heard other things. He heard tiny rustlings above him in the well, which made him wonder if things might fall down into his hair. He was thinking of insects. He heard wind blow over the well mouth, and that sound made an impression on him, too. In short, everything about his life was different for him at the bottom of that well. But nothing fell on him and nothing closed off that little circle of blue. Then his dad came along with the rope, and it wasn't long before J.P. was back in the world he'd always lived in.

"Keep talking, J.P. Then what?" I say.

When he was eighteen or nineteen years old and out of high school and had nothing whatsoever he wanted to do with his life, he went across town one afternoon to visit a friend. This friend lived in a house with a fireplace. J.P. and his friend sat around drinking beer and batting the breeze. They played some records. Then the doorbell rings. The friend goes to the door. This young woman chimney sweep is there with her cleaning things. She's wearing a top hat, the sight of which knocked J.P. for a loop. She tells J.P.'s friend that she has an appointment to clean the fireplace. The friend lets her in and bows. The young woman doesn't pay him any mind. She spreads a blanket on the hearth and lays out her gear. She's wearing these black pants, black shirt, black shoes and socks. Of course, by now she's taken her hat off. J.P. says it nearly drove him nuts to look at her. She does the work, she cleans the chimney, while J.P. and his friend play records and drink beer. But they watch her and they watch what she does. Now and then J.P. and his friend look at each other and grin, or else they wink. They raise their eyebrows when the upper half of the young woman disappears into the chimney. She was all-right-looking, too, J. P. said.

When she'd finished her work, she rolled her things up in the blanket. From J.P.'s friend, she took a check that had been made out to her by his parents. And then she asks the friend if he wants to kiss her. "It's supposed to bring good luck," she says. That does it for J.P. The friend rolls his eyes. He clowns some more. Then, probably blushing, he kisses her on the cheek. At this minute, J.P. made his mind up about something. He put his beer down. He got up from the sofa. He went over to the young woman as she was starting to go out the door.

"Me, too?" J. P. said to her.

She swept her eyes over him. J. P. says he could feel his heart knocking. The young woman's name, it turns out, was Roxy.

"Sure," Roxy says. "Why not? I've got some extra kisses." And she kissed him a good one right on the lips and then turned to go.

Like that, quick as a wink, J. P. followed her onto the porch. He held the porch screen door for her. He went down the steps with her and out to the drive, where she'd parked her panel truck. It was something that was out of his hands. Nothing else in the world counted for anything. He knew he'd met somebody who could set his legs atremble. He could feel her kiss still burning on his lips, etc. J. P. couldn't begin to sort anything out. He was filled with sensations that were carrying him every which way.

He opened the rear door of the panel truck for her. He helped her store her things inside. "Thanks," she told him. Then he blurted it out – that he'd like to see her again. Would she go to a movie with him sometime? He'd realized, too, what he wanted to do with his life. He wanted to do what she did. He wanted to be a chimney sweep. But he didn't tell her that then.

J.P. says she put her hands on her hips and looked him over. Then she found a business card in the front seat of her truck. She gave it to him. She said, "Call this number after ten tonight. We can talk. I have to go now." She put the top hat on and then took it off. She looked at J.P. once more. She must have liked what she saw, because this time she grinned. He told her there was a smudge near her mouth. Then she got into her truck, tooted the horn, and drove away.

"Then what?" I say. "Don't stop now, J.P."

I was interested. But I would have listened if he'd been going on about how one day he'd decided to start pitching horseshoes.

It rained last night. The clouds are banked up against the hills across the valley. J.P. clears his throat and looks at the hills and the clouds. He pulls his chin. Then he goes on with what he was saying.

Roxy starts going out with him on dates. And little by little he talks her into letting him go along on jobs with her.

But Roxy's in business with her father and brother and they've got just the right amount of work. They don't need anybody else. Besides, who was this guy J.P.? J.P. what? Watch out, they warned her.

So she and J.P. saw some movies together. They went to a few dances. But mainly the courtship revolved around their cleaning chimneys together. Before you know it, J.P. says, they're talking about tying the knot. And after a while they do it, they get married. J.P.'s new father-in-law takes him in as a full partner. In a year or so, Roxy has a kid. She's quit being a chimney sweep. At any rate, she's quit doing the work. Pretty soon she has another kid. J.P.'s in his mid-twenties by now. He's buying a house. He says he was happy with his life. "I was happy with the way things were going," he says. "I had everything I wanted. I had a wife and kids I loved, and I was doing what I wanted to do with my life." But for some reason – who knows why we do what we do? – his drinking picks up. For a long time he drinks beer and beer only. Any kind of beer – it didn't matter. He says he could drink beer twenty-four hours a day. He'd drink beer at night while he watched TV. Sure, once in a while he drank hard stuff. But that was only if they went out on the town, which was not often, or else when they had company over. Then a time comes, he doesn't know why, when he makes the switch from beer to gin-and-tonic. And he'd have more gin-and-tonic after dinner, sitting in front of the TV. There was always a glass of gin-and-tonic in his hand. He says he actually liked the taste of it. He began stopping off after work for drinks before he went home to have more drinks. Then he began missing some dinners. He just wouldn't show up. Or else he'd show up, but he wouldn't want anything to eat. He'd filled up on snacks at the bar. Sometimes he'd walk in the door and for no good reason throw his lunch pail across the living room. When Roxy yelled at him, he'd turn around and go out again. He moved his drinking time up to early afternoon, while he was still supposed to be working. He tells me that he was starting off the morning with a couple of drinks. He'd have a belt of the stuff before he brushed his teeth. Then he'd have his coffee. He'd go to work with a thermos bottle of vodka in his lunch pail.

J.P. quits talking. He just clams up. What's going on? I'm listening. It's helping me relax, for one thing. It's taking me away from my own situation. After a minute, I say, "What the hell? Go on, J.P." He's pulling his chin. But pretty soon he starts talking again.

J.P. and Roxy are having some real fights now. I mean *fights*. J.P. says that one time she hit him in the face with her fist and broke his nose. "Look at this," he says. "Right here." He shows me a line across the bridge of his nose. "That's a broken nose." He returned the favor. He dislocated her shoulder for her. Another time he split her lip. They beat on each other in front of the kids. Things got out of hand. But he kept on drinking. He couldn't stop. And nothing could make him stop. Not even with Roxy's dad and her brother threatening to beat the hell out of him. They told Roxy she should take the kids and clear out. But Roxy said it was her problem. She got herself into it, and she'd solve it.

Now J.P gets real quiet again. He hunches his shoulders and pulls down in his chair. He watches a car driving down the road between this place and the hills.

I say, "I want to hear the rest of this, J.P. You better keep talking."

"I just don't know," he says. He shrugs.

"It's all right," I say. And I mean it's okay for him to tell it. "Go on, J.P."

One way she tried to fix things, J.P. says, was by finding a boyfriend. J.P. would like to know how she found the time with the house and kids.

I look at him and I'm surprised. He's a grown man. "If you want to do that," I say, "you find the time. You make the time."

J.P. shakes his head. "I guess so," he says.

Anyway, he found out about it – about Roxy's boyfriend – and he went wild. He manages to get Roxy's wedding ring off her finger. And when he does, he cuts it into several pieces with a pair of wire-cutters. Good, solid fun. They'd already gone a couple of rounds on this occasion. On his way to work the next morning, he gets arrested on a drunk charge. He loses his driver's license. He can't drive the truck to work anymore. Just as well, he says. He'd already fallen off a roof the week before and broken his thumb. It was just a matter of time until he broke his neck, he says.

He was here at Frank Martin's to dry out and to figure how to get his life back on track. But he wasn't here against his will, any more than I was. We weren't locked up. We could leave any time we wanted. But a minimum stay of a week was recommended, and two weeks or a month was, as they put it, "strongly advised."

As I said, this is my second time at Frank Martin's. When I was trying to sign a check to pay in advance for a week's stay, Frank Martin said, "The holidays are always bad. Maybe you should think of sticking around a little longer this time? Think in terms of a couple of weeks. Can you do a couple of weeks? Think about it, anyway. You don't have to decide anything right now," he said. He held his thumb on the check and I signed my name. Then I walked my girlfriend to the front door and said goodbye. "Goodbye," she said, and she lurched into the doorjamb and then onto the porch. It's late afternoon. It's raining. I go from the door to the window. I move the curtain and watch her drive away. She's in my car. She's drunk. But I'm drunk, too, and there's nothing I can do. I make it to a big chair that's close to the radiator, and I sit down. Some guys look up from their TV. Then they shift back to what they were watching. I just sit there. Now and then I look up at something that's happening on the screen.

Later that afternoon the front door banged open and J.P. was brought in between these two big guys – his father-in-law and brother-in-law, I find out afterward. They steered J.P. across the room. The old guy signed him in and gave Frank Martin a check. Then these two guys helped J.P. upstairs. I guess they put him to bed. Pretty soon the old guy and the other guy came downstairs and headed for the front door. They couldn't seem to get out of this place fast enough. It was like they couldn't wait to wash their hands of all this. I didn't blame them. Hell, no. I don't know how I'd act if I was in their shoes.

A day and a half later J.P. and I meet up on the front porch. We shake hands and comment on the weather. J.P. has a case of the shakes. We sit down and prop our feet up on the railing. We lean back in our chairs like we're just out there taking our ease, like we might be getting ready to talk about our bird dogs. That's when J.P. gets going with his story.

It's cold out, but not too cold. It's a little overcast. Frank Martin comes outside to finish his cigar. He has on a sweater buttoned all the way up. Frank Martin is short and heavy-set. He has curly grey hair and a small head. His head is too small for the rest of his body. Frank Martin puts the cigar in his mouth and stands with his arms crossed over his chest. He works that cigar in his mouth and looks across the valley. He stands there like a prize-fighter, like somebody who knows the score.

J.P. gets quiet again. I mean, he's hardly breathing. I toss my cigarette into the coal bucket and look hard at J.P., who scoots farther down in his chair. J.P. pulls up his collar. What the hell's going on? I wonder. Frank Martin uncrosses his arms and takes a puff on the cigar. He lets the smoke carry out of his mouth. Then he raises his chin toward the hills and says, "Jack London used to have a big place on the other side of this valley. Right over there behind that green hill you're looking at. But alcohol killed him. Let that be a lesson to you. He was a better man than any of us. But he couldn't handle the stuff, either." Frank Martin looks at what's left of his cigar. It's gone out. He tosses it into the bucket. "You guys want to read something while you're here, read that book of his, *The Call of the Wild*. You know the one I'm talking about? We have it inside if you want to read something. It's about this animal that's half dog and half wolf. End of sermon," he says, and then hitches his pants up and tugs his sweater down. "I'm going inside," he says. "See you at lunch."

"I feel like a bug when he's around," J.P. says. "He makes me feel like a bug." J.P. shakes his head. Then he says, "Jack London. What a name! I wish I had me a name like that. Instead of the name I got."

My wife brought me up here the first time. That's when we were still together, trying to make things work out. She brought me here and she stayed around for an hour or two, talking to Frank Martin in private. Then she left. The next morning Frank Martin got me aside and said, "We can help you. If you want help and want to listen to what we say." But I didn't know if they could help me or not. Part of me wanted help. But there was another part.

This time around, it was my girlfriend who drove me here. She was driving my car. She drove us through a rainstorm. We drank champagne all the way. We were both drunk when she pulled up in the drive. She intended to drop me off, turn around, and drive home again. She had things to do. One thing she had to do was to go to work the next day. She was a secretary. She had an okay job with this electronic-parts firm. She also had this mouthy teenaged son. I wanted her to get a room in town, spend the night, and then drive home. I don't know if she got the room or not. I haven't heard from her since she led me up the front steps the other day and walked me into Frank Martin's office and said, "Guess who's here."

But I wasn't mad at her. In the first place, she didn't have any idea what she was letting herself in for when she said I could stay with her after my wife asked me to leave. I felt sorry for her. The reason I felt sorry for her was that on the day before Christmas her Pap smear came back, and the news was not cheery. She'd have to go back to the doctor, and real soon. That kind of news was reason enough for both of us to start drinking. So what we did was get ourselves good and drunk. And on Christmas Day we were still drunk. We had to go out to a restaurant to eat, because she didn't feel like cooking. The two of us and her mouthy teenaged son opened some presents, and then we went to this steakhouse near her apartment. I wasn't hungry. I had some soup and a hot roll. I drank a bottle of wine with the soup. She drank some wine, too Then we started in on Bloody Marys. For the next couple of days, I didn't eat anything except salted nuts. But I drank a lot of bourbon. Then I said to her, "Sugar, I think I'd better pack up. I better go back to Frank Martin's."

She tried to explain to her son that she was going to be gone for a while and he'd have to get his own food. But right as we were going out the door, this mouthy kid screamed at us. He screamed, "The hell with you! I hope you never come back. I hope you kill yourselves!" Imagine this kid!

Before we left town, I had her stop at the package store, where I bought us the champagne. We stopped someplace else for plastic glasses. Then we picked up a bucket of fried chicken. We set out for Frank Martin's in this rainstorm, drinking and listening to music. She drove. I looked after the radio and poured. We tried to make a little party of it. But we were sad, too. There was that fried chicken, but we didn't eat any.

I guess she got home okay. I think I would have heard something if she didn't. But she hasn't called me, and I haven't called her. Maybe she's had some news about herself by now. Then again, maybe she hasn't heard anything. Maybe it was all a mistake. Maybe it was somebody else's smear. But she has my car, and I have things at her house. I know we'll be seeing each other again.

They clang an old farm bell here to call you for mealtime. J.P. and I get out of our chairs and we go inside. It's starting to get too cold on the porch, anyway. We can see our breath drifting out from us as we talk.

New Year's Eve morning I try to call my wife. There is no answer. It's okay. But even if it wasn't okay, what am I supposed to do? The last time we talked on the phone, a couple of weeks ago, we screamed at each other. I hung a few names on her. "Wet brain!" she said, and put the phone back where it belonged.

But I wanted to talk to her now. Something had to be done about my stuff. I still had things at her house, too.

One of the guys here is a guy who travels. He goes to Europe and places. That's what he says, anyway. Business, he says. He also says he has his drinking under control and he doesn't have any idea why he's here at Frank Martin's. But he doesn't remember getting here. He laughs about it, about his not remembering. "Anyone can have a blackout," he says. "That doesn't prove a thing." He's not a drunk – he tells us this and we listen. "That's a serious charge to make," he says. "That kind of talk can ruin a good man's prospects." He says that if he'd only stick to whiskey and water, no ice, he'd never have these blackouts. It's the ice they put into your drink that does it. "Who do you know in Egypt?" he asks me. "I can use a few names over there."

For New Year's Eve dinner Frank Martin serves steak and baked potato. My appetite's coming back. I clean up everything on my plate and I could eat more. I look over at Tiny's plate. Hell, he's hardly touched a thing. His steak is just sitting there. Tiny is not the same old Tiny. The poor bastard had planned to be at home tonight. He'd planned to be in his robe and slippers in front of the TV, holding hands with his wife. Now he's afraid to leave. I can understand. One seizure means you're ready for another. Tiny hasn't told any more nutty stories on himself since it happened. He's stayed quiet and kept to himself. I ask him if I can have his steak, and he pushes his plate over to me.

Some of us are still up, sitting around the TV, watching Times Square, when Frank Martin comes in to show us his cake. He brings it around and shows it to each of us. I know he didn't make it. It's just a bakery cake. But it's still a cake. It's a big white cake. Across the top there's writing in pink letters. The writing says, HAPPY NEW YEAR – ONE DAY AT A TIME.

"I don't want any stupid cake," says the guy who goes to Europe and places. "Where's the champagne?" he says, and laughs.

We all go into the dining room. Frank Martin cuts the cake. I sit next to J.P. J.P. eats two pieces and drinks a Coke. I eat a piece and wrap another piece in a napkin, thinking of later.

J.P. lights a cigarette – his hands are steady now – and he tells me his wife is coming in the morning, the first day of the new year.

"That's great," I say. I nod. I lick the frosting off my finger. "That's good news, J.P."

"I'll introduce you," he says.

"I look forward to it," I say.

We say goodnight. We say Happy New Year. I use a napkin on my fingers. We shake hands.

I go to the phone, put in a dime, and call my wife collect. But nobody answers this time, either. I think about calling my girlfriend, and I'm dialing her number when I realize I really don't want to talk to her. She's probably at home watching the same thing on TV that I've been watching. Anyway, I don't want to talk to her. I hope she's okay. But if she has something wrong with her, I don't want to know about it.

After breakfast, J.P. and I take coffee out to the porch. The sky is clear, but it's cold enough for sweaters and jackets.

"She asked me if she should bring the kids," J.P. says. "I told her she should keep the kids at home. Can you imagine? My God, I don't want my kids up here."

We use the coal bucket for an ashtray. We look across the valley to where Jack London used to live. We're drinking more coffee when this car turns off the road and comes down the drive.

"That's her!" J.P. says. He puts his cup next to his chair. He gets up and goes down the steps.

I see this woman stop the car and set the brake. I see J.P. open the door. I watch her get out, and I see them hug each other. I look away. Then I look back. J.P. takes her by the arm and they come up the stairs. This woman broke a man's nose once. She has had two kids, and much trouble, but she loves this man who has her by the arm. I get up from the chair.

"This is my friend," J.P. says to his wife. "Hey, this is Roxy."

Roxy takes my hand. She's a tall, good-looking woman in a knit cap. She has on a coat, a heavy sweater, and slacks.

I recall what J.P. told me about the boyfriend and the wire-cutters. I don't see any wedding ring. That's in pieces somewhere, I guess. Her hands are broad and the fingers have these big knuckles. This is a woman who can make fists if she has to.

"I've heard about you," I say. "J.P. told me how you got acquainted. Something about a chimney, J.P. said."

"Yes, a chimney," she says. "There's probably a lot else he didn't tell you," she says. "I bet he didn't tell you everything," she says, and laughs. Then — she can't wait any longer — she slips her arm around J.P. and kisses him on the cheek. They start to move to the door. "Nice meeting you," she says. "Hey, did he tell you he's the best sweep in the business?"

"Come on now, Roxy," J.P. says. He has his hand on the doorknob.

"He told me he learned everything he knew from you," I say.

"Well, that much is sure true," she says. She laughs again. But it's like she's thinking about something else. J.P. turns the doorknob. Roxy lays her hand over his. "Joe, can't we go into town for lunch? Can't I take you someplace?"

J.P. clears his throat. He says, "It hasn't been a week yet." He takes his hand off the doorknob and brings his fingers to his chin. "I think they'd like it if I didn't leave the place for a little while yet. We can have some coffee here," he says.

"That's fine," she says. Her eyes work over to me again. "I'm glad Joe's made a friend. Nice to meet you," she says.

They start to go inside. I know it's a dumb thing to do, but I do it anyway. "Roxy," I say. And they stop in the doorway and look at me. "I need some luck," I say. "No kidding. I could do with a kiss myself."

J.P. looks down. He's still holding the knob, even though the door is open. He turns the knob back and forth. But I keep looking at her. Roxy grins. "I'm not a sweep anymore," she says. "Not for years. Didn't Joe tell you that? But, sure, I'll kiss you, sure."

She moves over. She takes me by the shoulders – I'm a big man – and she plants this kiss on my lips. "How's that?" she says.

"That's fine," I say.

"Nothing to it," she says. She's still holding me by the shoulders. She's looking me right in the eyes. "Good luck," she says, and then she lets go of me.

"See you later, pal," J.P. says. He opens the door all the way, and they go in.

I sit down on the front steps and light a cigarette. I watch what my hand does, then I blow out the match. I've got the shakes. I started out with them this morning. This morning I wanted something to drink. It's depressing, but I didn't say anything about it to J.P. I try to put my mind on something else.

I'm thinking about chimney sweeps – all that stuff I heard from J. P. – when for some reason I start to think about a house my wife and I once lived in. That house didn't have a chimney, so I don't know what makes me remember it now. But I remember the house and how we'd only been in there a few weeks when I heard a noise outside one morning. It was Sunday morning and it was still dark in the bedroom. But there was this pale light coming in from the bedroom window. I listened. I could hear something scrape against the side of the house. I jumped out of bed and went to look.

"My God!" my wife says, sitting up in bed and shaking the hair away from her face. Then she starts to laugh. "It's Mr Venturini," she says. "I forgot to tell you. He said he was coming to paint the house today. Early. Before it gets too hot.

I forgot all about it," she says, and laughs. "Come on back to bed, honey. It's just him."

"In a minute," I say.

I push the curtain away from the window. Outside, this old guy in white coveralls is standing next to his ladder. The sun is just starting to break above the mountains. The old guy and I look each other over. It's the landlord, all right – this old guy in coveralls. But his coveralls are too big for him. He needs a shave, too. And he's wearing this baseball cap to cover his bald head. Goddamn it, I think, if he isn't a weird old fellow. And a wave of happiness comes over me that I'm not him – that I'm me and that I'm inside this bedroom with my wife.

He jerks his thumb toward the sun. He pretends to wipe his forehead. He's letting me know he doesn't have all that much time. The old fart breaks into a grin. It's then I realize I'm naked. I look down at myself. I look at him again and shrug. What did he expect?

My wife laughs. "Come *on*," she says. "Get back in this bed. Right now. This minute. Come on back to bed."

I let go of the curtain. But I keep standing there at the window. I can see the old fellow nod to himself like he's saying, "Go on, sonny, go back to bed. I understand." He tugs on the bill of his cap. Then he sets about his business. He picks up his bucket. He starts climbing the ladder.

I lean back into the step behind me now and cross one leg over the other. Maybe later this afternoon I'll try calling my wife again. And then I'll call to see what's happening with my girlfriend. But I don't want to get her mouthy kid on the line. If I do call, I hope he'll be out somewhere doing whatever he does when he's not around the house. I try to remember if I ever read any Jack London books. I can't remember. But there was a story of his I read in high school. "To Build a Fire," it was called. This guy in the Yukon is freezing. Imagine it – he's actually going to freeze to death if he can't get a fire going. With a fire, he can dry his socks and things and warm himself.

He gets his fire going, but then something happens to it. A branchful of snow drops on it. It goes out. Meanwhile, it's getting colder. Night is coming on.

I bring some change out of my pocket. I'll try my wife first. If she answers, I'll wish her a Happy New Year. But that's it. I won't bring up business. I won't raise my voice. Not even if she starts something. She'll ask me where I'm calling from, and I'll have to tell her. I won't say anything about New Year's resolutions. There's no way to make a joke out of this. After I talk to her, I'll call my girlfriend. Maybe I'll call her first. I'll just have to hope I don't get her kid on the line. "Hello, sugar," I'll say when she answers. "It's me."

The Train

FOR JOHN CHEEVER

The woman was called Miss Dent, and earlier that evening she'd held a gun on a man. She'd made him get down in the dirt and plead for his life. While the man's eyes welled with tears and his fingers picked at leaves, she pointed the revolver at him and told him things about himself. She tried to make him see that he couldn't keep trampling on people's feelings. "Be still!" she'd said, although the man was only digging his fingers into the dirt and moving his legs a little out of fear. When she had finished talking, when she had said all she could think of to say to him, she put her foot on the back of his head and pushed his face into the dirt. Then she put the revolver into her handbag and walked back to the railway station.

She sat on a bench in the deserted waiting room with the handbag on her lap. The ticket office was closed; no one was around. Even the parking lot outside the station was empty. She let her eyes rest on the big wall clock. She wanted to stop thinking about the man and how he'd acted toward her after taking what he wanted. But she knew she would remember for a long time the sound he made through his nose as he got down on his knees. She took a breath, closed her eyes, and listened for the sound of a train.

The waiting-room door opened. Miss Dent looked in that direction as two people came inside. One person was an old man with white hair and a white silk cravat; the other was a middle-aged woman wearing eye-shadow, lipstick, and a rose-colored knit dress. The evening had turned cool, but neither of the people wore a coat, and the old man was without shoes. They stopped in the doorway, seemingly astounded at finding someone in the waiting room. They tried to act as if her presence there was not a disappointment The woman said something to the old man, but Miss Dent didn't catch what it was the woman had said. The couple moved on into the room. It seemed to Miss Dent that they gave off an air of agitation, of having just left somewhere in a great hurry and not yet being able to find a way to talk about it. It might be, Miss Dent thought, that they'd had too much to drink as well. The woman and the white-haired old man looked at the clock, as if it might tell them some-thing about their situation and what they were supposed to do next.

Miss Dent also turned her eyes to the clock. There was nothing in the waiting room that announced when trains arrived and departed. But she was prepared to wait for any length of time. She knew if she waited long enough, a train would come along, and she could board it, and it would take her away from this place.

"Good evening," the old man said to Miss Dent. He said this, she thought, as if it had been a normal summer's night and he were an important old man wearing shoes and an evening jacket.

"Good evening," Miss Dent said.

The woman in the knit dress looked at her in a way that was calculated to let Miss Dent know the woman was not happy at finding her in the waiting room.

The old man and the woman seated themselves on a bench directly across the lobby from Miss Dent. She watched as the old man gave the knees of his trousers a little tug and then crossed one leg over the other and began to wag his stockinged foot. He took a pack of cigarettes and a cigarette holder from his shirt pocket. He inserted the cigarette into the holder and brought his hand up to his shirt pocket. Then he reached into his trouser pockets.

"I don't have a light," he said to the woman.

"I don't smoke," the woman said. "I should think if you knew anything about me, you'd know that much. If you really must smoke, *she* may have a match." The woman raised her chin and looked sharply at Miss Dent.

But Miss Dent shook her head. She pulled the handbag closer. She held her knees together, her fingers gripping the bag.

"So on top of everything else, no matches," the white-haired old man said. He checked his pockets once more. Then he sighed and removed the cigarette from the holder. He pushed the cigarette back into the pack. He put the cigarettes and the cigarette holder into his shirt pocket.

The woman began to speak in a language that Miss Dent did not understand. She thought it might be Italian because the rapid-fire words sounded like words she'd heard Sophia Loren use in a film. The old man shook his head. "I can't follow you, you know. You're going too fast for me. You'll have to slow down. You'll have to speak English. I can't follow you," he said.

Miss Dent released her grasp on the handbag and moved it from her lap to a place next to her on the bench. She stared at the catch on the handbag. She wasn't sure what she should do. It was a small waiting room, and she hated to get up suddenly and move somewhere else to sit. Her eyes traveled to the clock.

"I can't get over that bunch of nuts back there," the woman said. "It's colossal! It's simply too much for words.

My God!" The woman said this and shook her head. She slumped against the bench as if exhausted. She raised her eyes and stared briefly at the ceiling.

The old man took the silk cravat between his fingers and began idly to rub the material back and forth. He opened a button on his shirt and tucked the cravat inside. He seemed to be thinking about something else as the woman went on.

"It's that girl I feel sorry for," the woman said. "That poor soul alone in a house filled with simps and vipers. She's the one I feel sorry for. And she'll be the one to pay! None of the rest of them. Certainly not that imbecile they call Captain Nick! He isn't responsible for anything. Not him," the woman said.

The old man raised his eyes and looked around the waiting room. He gazed for a time at Miss Dent.

Miss Dent looked past his shoulder and through the window. There she could see the tall lamp post, its light shining on the empty parking lot. She held her hands together in her lap and tried to keep her attention on her own affairs. But she couldn't help hearing what these people said.

"I can tell you this much," the woman said. "The girl is the extent of my concern. Who cares about the rest of that tribe? Their entire existence is taken up with *café au lait* and cigarettes, their precious Swiss chocolate and those goddamned macaws. Nothing else means anything to them," the woman said. "What do they care? If I never see that outfit again, it'll be too soon. Do you understand me?"

"Sure, I understand," the old man said. "Of course." He put his feet on the floor and then brought his other leg up over his knee. "But don't fret about it now," he said.

" 'Don't fret about it,' he says. Why don't you take a look at yourself in the mirror?" the woman said.

"Don't worry about me," the old man said. "Worse things

have happened to me, and I'm still here." He laughed quietly and shook his head. "Don't worry about me."

"How can I help not worrying about you?" the woman said. "Who else is going to worry about you? Is this woman with the handbag going to worry about you?" she said, stopping long enough to glare at Miss Dent. "I'm serious, *amico mio*. Just look at yourself! My God, if I didn't already have so many things on my mind, I could have a nervous breakdown right here. Tell me who else there is to worry about you if I don't worry? I'm asking a serious question. You know so much," the woman said, "so answer me that."

The white-haired old man got to his feet and then sat down again. "Just don't worry about me," he said. "Worry about someone else. Worry about the girl and Captain Nick, if you want to worry. You were in another room when he said, 'I'm not serious, but I'm in love with her.' Those were his exact words."

"I knew something like that was coming!" the woman cried. She closed her fingers and brought her hands up to her temples. "I knew you'd tell me something like that! But I'm not surprised, either. No, I'm not. A leopard doesn't change its spots. Truer words were never spoken. Live and learn. But when are you going to wake up, you old fool? Answer me that," she said to him. "Are you like the mule that first has to be hit between the eyes with a two-by-four? *O Dio mio!* Why don't you go look at yourself in the mirror?" the woman said. "Take a good long look while you're at it."

The old man got up from the bench and moved over to the drinking fountain. He put one hand behind his back, turned the knob, and bent over to drink. Then he straightened up and dabbed his chin with the back of his hand.

He put both hands behind his back and began to stroll around the waiting room as if he were on a promenade.

But Miss Dent could see his eyes scanning the floor, the empty benches, the ashtrays. She understood he was looking for matches, and she was sorry she didn't have any.

The woman had turned to follow the old man's progress. She raised her voice and said: "Kentucky Fried Chicken at the North Pole! Colonel Sanders in a parka and boots. That tore it! That was the limit!"

The old man didn't answer. He continued his circum-navigation of the room and came to a stop at the front window. He stood at the window, hands behind his back, and looked out onto the empty parking lot.

The woman turned around to Miss Dent. She pulled at the material under the arm of her dress. "The next time I want to see home movies about Point Barrow, Alaska, and its native American Eskimos, I'll ask for them. My God, it was priceless! Some people will go to any lengths. Some people will try to kill their enemies with boredom. But you'd have needed to be there." The woman stared hotly at Miss Dent as if daring her to contradict.

Miss Dent picked up the handbag and placed it on her lap. She looked at the clock, which seemed to be moving very slowly, if at all.

"You don't say much," the woman said to Miss Dent. "But I'll wager you could say a lot if someone got you started. Couldn't you? But you're a sly boots. You'd rather just sit with your prim little mouth while other people talk their heads off. Am I right? Still waters. Is that your name?" the woman asked. "What *do* they call you?"

"Miss Dent. But I don't know you," Miss Dent said.

"I sure as hell don't know you, either!" the woman said. "Don't know you and don't care to know you. Sit there and think what you want. It won't change anything. But I know what I think, and I think it stinks!"

The old man left his place at the window and went outside. When he came back in a minute later, he had a cigarette burning in his holder and he seemed in better spirits. He carried his shoulders back and his chin out. He sat down beside the woman.

"I found some matches," he said. "There they were, a book of matches right next to the curb. Someone must have dropped them."

"Basically, you're lucky," the woman said. "And that's a plus in your situation. I always knew that about you, even if no one else did. Luck is important." The woman looked over at Miss Dent and said: "Young lady, I'll wager you've had your share of trial and error in this life. I know you have. The expression on your face tells me so. But you aren't going to talk about it. Go ahead then, don't talk. Let us do the talking. But you'll get older. Then you'll have something to talk about. Wait until you're my age. Or his age," the woman said and jerked her thumb at the old man. "God forbid. But it'll all come to you. In its own sweet time, it'll come. You won't have to hunt for it, either. It'll find you."

Miss Dent got up from the bench with her handbag and went over to the water fountain. She drank from the fountain and turned to look at them. The old man had finished smoking. He took what was left of his cigarette from the holder and dropped it under the bench. He tapped the holder against his palm, blew into the mouthpiece, and returned the holder to his shirt pocket. Now he, too, gave his attention to Miss Dent. He fixed his eyes on her and waited along with the woman. Miss Dent gathered herself to speak. She wasn't sure where to begin, but she thought she might start by saying she had a gun in her handbag.

She might even tell them she'd nearly killed a man earlier that night.

But at that moment they heard the train. First they heard the whistle, then a clanging sound, an alarm bell, as the guard rails went down at the crossing. The woman and the white-haired old man got up from the bench and moved toward the door. The old man opened the door for his companion, and then he smiled and made a little movement with his fingers for Miss Dent to precede him. She held the hand-bag against the front of her blouse and followed the older woman outside.

The train tooted its whistle once more as it slowed and then ground to a stop in front of the station. The light on the cab of the engine went back and forth over the track. The two cars that made up this little train were well lighted, so it was easy for the three people on the platform to see that the train was nearly empty. But this didn't surprise them. At this hour, they were surprised to see anyone at all on the train.

The few passengers in the cars looked out through the glass and thought it strange to find these people on the platform; making ready to board a train at this time of night. What business could have taken them out? This was the hour when people should be thinking of going to bed. The kitchens in the houses up on the hills behind the station were clean and orderly; the dishwashers had long ago finished their cycle, all things were in their places. Night-lights burned in children's bedrooms. A few teen-aged girls might still be reading novels, their fingers twisting a strand of hair as they did so. But television sets were going off now. Husbands and wives were making their own preparations for the night. The half-dozen or so passengers, sitting by themselves in the two cars, looked through the glass and wondered about the three people on the platform.

They saw a heavily made-up, middle-aged woman wearing a rose-colored knit dress mount the steps and enter the train. Behind her came a younger woman dressed in a summer blouse and skirt who clutched a handbag. They were followed onto the train by an old man who moved slowly and who carried himself in a dignified manner. The old man had white hair and a white silk cravat, but he was without shoes. The passengers naturally assumed that the three people boarding were together; and they felt sure that whatever these people's business had been that night, it had not come to a happy conclusion. But the passengers had seen things more various than this in their lifetime. The world is filled with business of every sort, as they well knew. This still was not as bad, perhaps, as it could be. For this reason, they scarcely gave another thought to these three who moved down the aisle and took up their places – the woman and the white-haired old man next to each other, the young woman with the handbag a few seats behind. Instead, the passengers gazed out at the station and went back to thinking about their own business, those things that had engaged them before the station stop.

The conductor looked up the track. Then he glanced back in the direction the train had come from. He raised his arm and, with his lantern, signaled the engineer. This was what the engineer was waiting for. He turned a dial and pushed down on a lever. The train began to move forward. It went slowly at first, but it began to pick up speed. It moved faster until once more it sped through the dark countryside, its brilliant cars throwing light onto the roadbed.

Fever

Carlyle was in a spot. He'd been in a spot all summer, since early June when his wife had left him. But up until a little while ago, just a few days before he had to start meeting his classes at the high school, Carlyle hadn't needed a sitter. He'd been the sitter. Every day and every night he'd attended to the children. Their mother, he told them, was away on a long trip.

Debbie, the first sitter he contacted, was a fat girl, nineteen years old, who told Carlyle she came from a big family. Kids loved her, she said. She offered a couple of names for reference. She penciled them on a piece of notebook paper. Carlyle took the names, folded the piece of paper, and put it in his shirt pocket. He told her he had meetings the next day. He said she could start to work for him the next morning. She said, "Okay."

He understood that his life was entering a new period. Eileen had left while Carlyle was still filling out his grade reports. She'd said she was going to Southern California to begin a new life for herself there. She'd gone with Richard Hoopes, one of Carlyle's colleagues at the high school. Hoopes was a drama teacher and glass-blowing instructor who'd apparently turned his grades in on time, taken his things, and left town in a hurry with Eileen. Now, the long and painful summer nearly behind him, and his classes about to resume, Carlyle had finally turned his attention to this matter of finding a baby-sitter. His first efforts had not been successful. In his desperation to find someone – anyone – he'd taken Debbie on.

In the beginning, he was grateful to have this girl turn up in response to his call. He'd yielded up the house and children to her as if she were a relative. So he had no one to blame but himself, his own carelessness, he was convinced, when he came home early from school one day that first week and pulled into the drive next to a car that had a big pair of flannel dice hanging from the rearview mirror. To his astonishment, he saw his children in the front yard, their clothes filthy, playing with a dog big enough to bite off their hands. His son, Keith, had the hiccups and had been crying. Sarah, his daughter, began to cry when she saw him get out of the car. They were sitting on the grass, and the dog was licking their hands and faces. The dog growled at him and then moved off a little as Carlyle made for his children. He picked up Keith and then he picked up Sarah. One child under each arm, he made for his front door. Inside the house, the phonograph was turned up so high the front windows vibrated.

In the living room, three teenaged boys jumped to their feet from where they'd been sitting around the coffee table.

Beer bottles stood on the table and cigarettes burned in the ashtray. Rod Stewart screamed from the stereo. On the sofa, Debbie, the fat girl, sat with another teenaged boy. She stared at Carlyle with dumb disbelief as he entered the living room. The fat girl's blouse was unbuttoned. She had her legs drawn under her, and she was smoking a cigarette. The living room was filled with smoke and music. The fat girl and her friend got off the sofa in a hurry.

"Mr Carlyle, wait a minute," Debbie said. "I can explain."

"Don't explain," Carlyle said. "Get the hell out of here. All of you. Before I throw you out." He tightened his grip on the children.

"You owe me for four days," the fat girl said, as she tried to button her blouse. She still had the cigarette between her fingers. Ashes fell from the cigarette as she tried to button up. "Forget today. You don't owe me for today. Mr Carlyle, it's not what it looks like. They dropped by to listen to this record."

"I understand, Debbie," he said. He let the children down onto the carpet. But they stayed close to his legs and watched the people in the living room. Debbie looked at them and shook her head slowly, as if she'd never laid eyes on them before. "Goddamn it, get out!" Carlyle said. "Now. Get going. All of you."

He went over and opened the front door. The boys acted as if they were in no real hurry. They picked up their beer and started slowly for the door. The Rod Stewart record was still playing. One of them said, "That's my record."

"Get it," Carlyle said. He took a step toward the boy and then stopped.

"Don't touch me, okay? Just don't touch me," the boy said. He went over to the phonograph, picked up the arm, swung it back, and took his record off while the turntable was still spinning.

Carlyle's hands were shaking. "If that car's not out of the drive in one minute – one minute – I'm calling the police." He felt sick and dizzy with his anger. He saw, really saw, spots dance in front of his eyes.

"Hey, listen, we're on our way, all right? We're going," the boy said.

They filed out of the house. Outside, the fat girl stumbled a little. She weaved as she moved toward the car. Carlyle saw her stop and bring her hands up to her face. She stood like that in the drive for a minute. Then one of the boys pushed her from behind and said her name. She dropped her hands and got into the back seat of the car.

"Daddy will get you into some clean clothes," Carlyle told his children, trying to keep his voice steady. "I'll give you a bath, and put you into some clean clothes. Then we'll go out for some pizza. How does pizza sound to you?"

"Where's Debbie?" Sarah asked him.

"She's gone," Carlyle said.

That evening, after he'd put the children to bed, he called Carol, the woman from school he'd been seeing for the last month. He told her what had happened with his sitter.

"My kids were out in the yard with this big dog," he said. "The dog was as big as a wolf. The baby-sitter was in the house with a bunch of her hoodlum boyfriends. They had Rod Stewart going full blast, and they were tying one on while my kids were outside with this strange dog." He brought his fingers to his temples and held them there while he talked.

"My God," Carol said. "Poor sweetie, I'm so sorry." Her voice sounded indistinct. He pictured her letting the receiver slide down to her chin, as she was in the habit of doing while talking on the phone. He'd seen her do it before. It was a habit of hers he found vaguely irritating. Did he want her to come over to his place? she asked. She would. She thought maybe she'd better do that. She'd call her sitter. Then she'd drive to his place. She wanted to. He shouldn't be afraid to say when he needed affection, she said. Carol was one of the secretaries in the principal's office at the high school where Carlyle taught art classes. She was divorced and had one child, a neurotic ten-year-old the father had named Dodge, after his automobile.

"No, that's all right," Carlyle said. "But thanks. *Thanks*, Carol. The kids are in bed, but I think I'd feel a little funny, you know, having company tonight."

She didn't offer again. "Sweetie, I'm sorry about what happened. But I understand your wanting to be alone tonight. I respect that. I'll see you at school tomorrow."

He could hear her waiting for him to say something else. "That's two baby-sitters in less than a week," he said. "I'm going out of my tree with this."

"Honey, don't let it get you down," she said. "Something will turn up. I'll help you find somebody this weekend. It'll be all right, you'll see."

"Thanks again for being there when I need you," he said. "You're one in a million, you know."

"'Night, Carlyle," she said.

After he'd hung up, he wished he could have thought of something else to say to her instead of what he'd just said. He'd never talked that way before in his life. They weren't having a love affair, he wouldn't call it that, but he liked her. She knew it was a hard time for him, and she didn't make demands.

After Eileen had left for California, Carlyle had spent every waking minute for the first month with his children. He supposed the shock of her going had caused this, but he didn't want to let the children out of his sight. He'd certainly not been interested in seeing other women, and for a time he didn't think he ever would be. He felt as if he were in mourning. His days and nights were passed in the company of his children. He cooked for them – he had no appetite himself – washed and ironed their clothes, drove them into the country where they picked flowers and ate sandwiches wrapped up in waxed paper. He took them to the super-market and let them pick out what they liked. And every few days they went to the park, or else to the library, or the zoo. They took old bread to the zoo so they could feed the ducks. At night, before tucking them in, Carlyle read to them – Aesop, Hans Christian Andersen, the Brothers Grimm.

"When is Mama coming back?" one of them might ask him in the middle of a fairy tale.

"Soon," he'd say. "One of these days. Now listen to this." Then he'd read the tale to its conclusion, kiss them, and turn off the light.

And while they'd slept, he had wandered the rooms of his house with a glass in his hand, telling himself that, yes, sooner or later, Eileen would come back. In the next breath, he would say, "I never want to see your face again. I'll never forgive you for this, you crazy bitch." Then, a minute later, "Come back, sweetheart, please. I love you and need you. The kids need you, too." Some nights that summer he fell asleep in front of the TV and woke up with the set still going and the screen filled with snow. This was the period when he didn't think he would be seeing any women for a long time, if ever. At night, sitting in front of the TV with an unopened book or magazine next to him on the sofa, he often thought of Eileen. When he did, he might remember her sweet laugh, or else her hand rubbing his neck if he complained of a soreness there. It was at these times that he thought he could weep. He thought, You hear about stuff like this happening to other people.

Just before the incident with Debbie, when some of the shock and grief had worn off, he'd phoned an employment service to tell them something of his predicament and his requirements. Someone took down the information and said they would get back to him. Not many people wanted to do housework and baby-sit, they said, but they'd find somebody. A few days before he had to be at the high school for meetings and registration, he called again and was told there'd be somebody at his house first thing the next morning.

That person was a thirty-five-year-old woman with hairy arms and run-over shoes. She shook hands with him and listened to him talk without asking a single question about the children – not even their names. When he took her into the back of the house where the children were playing, she simply stared at them for a minute without saying anything. When she finally smiled, Carlyle noticed for the first time that she had a tooth missing. Sarah left her crayons and got up to come over and stand next to him. She took Carlyle's hand and stared at the woman. Keith stared at her, too. Then he went back to his coloring. Carlyle thanked the woman for her time and said he would be in touch.

That afternoon he took down a number from an index card tacked to the bulletin board at the supermarket. Someone was offering baby-sitting services. References furnished on request. Carlyle called the number and got Debbie, the fat girl.

Over the summer, Eileen had sent a few cards, letters, and photographs of herself to the children, and some pen-and-ink drawings of her own that she'd done since she'd gone away. She also sent Carlyle long, rambling letters in which she asked for his understanding in this matter – this *matter* – but told him that she was happy. Happy. As if, Carlyle thought, happiness was all there was to life. She told him that if he really loved her, as he said he did, and as she really believed – she loved him, too, don't forget – then he would understand and accept things as they were. She wrote, "That which is truly bonded can never become unbonded." Carlyle didn't know if she was talking about their own relationship or her way of life out in California. He hated the word *bonded*. What did it have to do with the two of them? Did she think they were a corporation? He thought Eileen must be losing her mind to talk like that. He read that part again and then crumpled the letter.

But a few hours later he retrieved the letter from the trash can where he'd thrown it, and put it with her other cards and letters in a box on the shelf in his closet. In one of the envelopes there was a photograph of her in a big, floppy hat, wearing a bathing suit. And there was a pencil drawing on heavy paper of a woman on a riverbank in a filmy gown, her hands covering her eyes, her shoulders slumped. It was, Carlyle assumed Eileen showing her heartbreak over the situation. In college, she had majored in art, and even though she'd agreed to marry him, she said she intended to do something with her talent.

Carlyle said he wouldn't have it any other way. She owed it to herself, he said. She owed it to both of them. They had loved each other in those days. He knew they had. He couldn't imagine ever loving anyone again the way he'd loved her. And he'd felt loved, too. Then, after eight years of being married to him, Eileen had pulled out. She was, she said in her letter, "going for it."

After talking to Carol, he looked in on the children, who were asleep. Then he went into the kitchen and made himself a drink. He thought of calling Eileen to talk to her about the baby-sitting crisis, but decided against it. He had her phone number and her address out there, of course. But he'd only called once and, so far, had not written a letter. This was partly out of a feeling of bewilderment with the situation, partly out of anger and humiliation. Once, earlier in the summer, after a few drinks, he'd chanced humiliation and called. Richard Hoopes answered the phone. Richard had said, "Hey, Carlyle," as if he were still Carlyle's friend. And then, as if remembering something, he said, "Just a minute, all right?"

Eileen had come on the line and said, "Carlyle, how are you? How are the kids? Tell me about yourself." He told her the kids were fine. But before he could say anything else, she interrupted him to say, "I know *they're* fine. What about *you*?" Then she went on to tell him that her head was in the right place for the first time in a long time. Next she wanted to talk about his head and his karma. She'd looked into his karma. It was going to improve any time now, she said. Carlyle listened, hardly able to believe his ears. Then he said, "I have to go now, Eileen." And he hung up. The phone rang a minute or so later, but he let it ring. When it stopped ringing, he took the phone off the hook and left it off until he was ready for bed.

He wanted to call her now, but he was afraid to call. He still missed her and wanted to confide in her. He longed to hear her voice sweet, steady, not manic as it had been for months now – but if he dialed her number, Richard Hoopes might answer the telephone. Carlyle knew he didn't want to hear that man's voice again. Richard had been a colleague for three years and, Carlyle supposed, a kind of friend. At least he was someone Carlyle ate lunch with in the faculty dining room, someone who talked about Tennessee Williams and the photographs of Ansel Adams. But even if Eileen answered the telephone, she might launch into something about his karma.

While he was sitting there with the glass in his hand, trying to remember what it had felt like to be married and intimate with someone, the phone rang. He picked up the receiver, heard a trace of static on the line, and knew, even before she'd said his name, that it was Eileen.

"I was just thinking about you," Carlyle said, and at once regretted saying it.

"See! I knew I was on your mind, Carlyle. Well, I was

thinking about you, too. That's why I called." He drew a breath. She was losing her mind. That much was clear to him. She kept talking. "Now listen," she said. "The big reason I called is that I know things are in kind of a mess out there right now. Don't ask me how, but I know. I'm sorry, Carlyle. But here's the thing. You're still in need of a good house-keeper and sitter combined, right? Well, she's practically right there in the neighborhood! Oh, you may have found someone already, and that's good, if that's the case. If so, it's supposed to be that way. But see, just in case you're having trouble in that area, there's this woman who used to work for Richard's mother. I told Richard about the potential problem, and he put himself to work on it. You want to know what he did? Are you listening? He called his mother, who used to have this woman who kept house for her. The woman's name is Mrs Webster. She looked after things for Richard's mother before his aunt and her daughter moved in there. Richard was able to get a number through his mother. He talked to Mrs Webster today. Richard did. Mrs Webster is going to call you tonight. Or else maybe she'll call you in the morning. One or the other. Anyway, she's going to volunteer her services, if you need her. You might, you never can tell. Even if your situation is okay right now, which I hope it is. But some time or another you might need her. You know what I'm saying? If not this minute, some other time. Okay? How are the kids? What are they up to?"

"The children are fine, Eileen. They're asleep now," he said. Maybe he should tell her they cried themselves to sleep every night. He wondered if he should tell her the truth — that they hadn't asked about her even once in the last couple of weeks. He decided not to say anything.

"I called earlier, but the line was busy. I told Richard you were probably talking to your girlfriend," Eileen said and laughed. "Think positive thoughts. You sound depressed," she said.

"I have to go, Eileen." He started to hang up, and he took the receiver from his ear. But she was still talking.

"Tell Keith and Sarah I love them. Tell them I'm sending some more pictures. Tell them that. I don't want them to forget their mother is an artist. Maybe not a great artist yet, that's not important. But, you know, an artist. It's important they shouldn't forget that."

Carlyle said, "I'll tell them."

"Richard says hello."

Carlyle didn't say anything. He said the word to himself – *hello*. What could the man possibly mean by this? Then he said, "Thanks for calling. Thanks for talking to that woman."

"Mrs Webster!"

"Yes. I'd better get off the phone now. I don't want to run up your nickel."

Eileen laughed. "It's only money. Money's not important except as a necessary medium of exchange. There are more important things than money. But then you already know that."

He held the receiver out in front of him. He looked at the instrument from which her voice was issuing.

"Carlyle, things are going to get better for you. I *know* they are. You may think I'm crazy or something," she said. "But just remember."

Remember what? Carlyle wondered in alarm, thinking he must have missed something she'd said. He brought the receiver in close. "Eileen, thanks for calling," he said.

"We have to stay in touch," Eileen said. "We have to keep all lines of communication open. I think the worst is over. For both of us. I've suffered, too. But we're going to get what we're supposed to get out of this life, both of us, and we're going to be made *stronger* for it in the long run."

"Goodnight," he said. He put the receiver back. Then he looked at the phone. He waited. It didn't ring again. But an hour later it did ring. He answered it.

"Mr Carlyle." It was an old woman's voice. "You don't know me, but my name is Mrs Jim Webster. I was supposed to get in touch."

"Mrs Webster. Yes," he said. Eileen's mention of the woman came back to him. "Mrs Webster, can you come to my house in the morning? Early. Say seven o'clock?"

"I can do that easily," the old woman said. "Seven o'clock. Give me your address."

"I'd like to be able to count on you," Carlyle said.

"You can count on me," she said.

"I can't tell you how important it is," Carlyle said.

"Don't you worry," the old woman said.

The next morning, when the alarm went off, he wanted to keep his eyes closed and keep on with the dream he was having. Something about a farmhouse. And there was a waterfall in there, too. Someone, he didn't know who, was walking along the road carrying something. Maybe it was a picnic hamper. He was not made uneasy by the dream. In the dream, there seemed to exist a sense of well-being.

Finally, he rolled over and pushed something to stop the buzzing. He lay in bed awhile longer. Then he got up, put his feet into his slippers, and went out to the kitchen to start the coffee.

He shaved and dressed for the day. Then he sat down at the kitchen table with coffee and a cigarette. The children were still in bed. But in five minutes or so he planned to put boxes of cereal on the table and lay out bowls and spoons, then go in to wake them for breakfast. He really couldn't believe that the old woman who'd phoned him last night would show up this morning, as she'd said she would. He decided he'd wait until five minutes after seven o'clock, and then he'd call in, take the day off, and make every effort in the book to locate someone reliable. He brought the cup of coffee to his lips.

It was then that he heard a rumbling sound out in the street. He left his cup and got up from the table to look out the window. A pickup truck had pulled over to the curb in front of his house. The pickup cab shook as the engine idled. Carlyle went to the front door, opened it, and waved. An old woman waved back and then let herself out of the vehicle. Carlyle saw the driver lean over and disappear under the dash. The truck gasped, shook itself once more, and fell still.

"Mr Carlyle?" the old woman said, as she came slowly up his walk carrying a large purse.

"Mrs Webster," he said. "Come on inside. Is that your husband? Ask him in. I just made coffee."

"It's okay," she said. "He has his thermos."

Carlyle shrugged. He held the door for her. She stepped inside and they shook hands. Mrs Webster smiled. Carlyle nodded. They moved out to the kitchen. "Did you want me today, then?" she asked.

"Let me get the children up," he said. "I'd like them to meet you before I leave for school."

"That'd be good," she said. She looked around his kitchen She put her purse on the drainboard.

"Why don't I get the children?" he said. "I'll just be a minute or two."

In a little while, he brought the children out and introduced them. They were still in their pyjamas. Sarah was rubbing her eyes. Keith was wide awake. "This is Keith,"

Carlyle said. "And this one here, this is my Sarah." He held on to Sarah's hand and turned to Mrs Webster. "They need someone, you see. We need someone we can count on. I guess that's our problem."

Mrs Webster moved over to the children. She fastened the top button or Keith's pyjamas. She moved the hair away from Sarah's face. They let her do it. "Don't you kids worry, now," she said to them. "Mr Carlyle, it'll be all right. We're going to be fine. Give us a day or two to get to know each other, that's all. But if I'm going to stay, why don't you give Mr Webster the all-clear sign? Just wave at him through the window," she said, and then she gave her attention back to the children.

Carlyle stepped to the bay window and drew the curtain. An old man was watching the house from the cab of the truck. He was just bringing a thermos cup to his lips. Carlyle waved to him, and with his free hand the man waved back. Carlyle watched him roll down the truck window and throw out what was left in his cup. Then he bent down under the dash again – Carlyle imagined him touching some wires together – and in a minute the truck started and began to shake. The old man put the truck in gear and pulled away from the curb.

Carlyle turned from the window. "Mrs Webster," he said, "I'm glad you're here."

"Likewise, Mr Carlyle," she said. "Now you go on about your business before you're late. Don't worry about anything. We're going to be fine. Aren't we, kids?"

The children nodded their heads. Keith held on to her dress with one hand. He put the thumb of his other hand into his mouth.

"Thank you," Carlyle said. "I feel, I really feel a hundred percent better." He shook his head and grinned. He felt a welling in his chest as he kissed each of his children goodbye. He told Mrs Webster what time she could expect him home, put on his coat, said goodbye once more, and went out of the house. For the first time in months, it seemed, he felt his burden had lifted a little. Driving to school, he listened to some music on the radio.

During first-period art-history class, he lingered over slides of Byzantine paintings. He patiently explained the nuances of detail and motif. He pointed out the emotional power and fitness of the work. But he took so long trying to place the anonymous artists in their social milieu that some of his students began to scrape their shoes on the floor, or else clear their throats. They covered only a third of the lesson plan that day. He was still talking when the bell rang.

In his next class, watercolor painting, he felt unusually calm and insightful. "Like this, like this," he said, guiding their hands. "Delicately. Like a breath of air on the paper. Just a touch. Like so. See?" he'd say and felt on the edge of discovery himself. "Suggestion is what it's all about," he said, holding lightly to Sue Colvin's fingers as he guided her brush. "You've got to work with your mistakes until they look intended. Understand?"

As he moved down the lunch line in the faculty dining room, he saw Carol a few places ahead of him. She paid for her food. He waited impatiently while his own bill was being rung up. Carol was halfway across the room by the time he caught up with her. He slipped his hand under her elbow and guided her to an empty table near the window.

"God, Carlyle," she said after they'd seated themselves. She picked up her glass of iced tea. Her face was flushed. "Did you see the look Mrs Storr gave us? What's wrong with you? Everybody will know." She sipped from her iced tea and put the glass down.

"The hell with Mrs Storr," Carlyle said. "Hey, let me tell you something. Honey, I feel light-years better than I did this time yesterday. Jesus," he said.

"What's happened?" Carol said. "Carlyle, tell me." She moved her fruit cup to one side of her tray and shook cheese over her spaghetti. But she didn't eat anything. She waited for him to go on. "Tell me what it is."

He told her about Mrs Webster. He even told her about Mr Webster. How the man'd had to hot-wire the truck in order to start it. Carlyle ate his tapioca while he talked. Then he ate the garlic bread. He drank Carol's iced tea down before he realized he was doing it.

"You're nuts, Carlyle," she said, nodding at the spaghetti in his plate that he hadn't touched.

He shook his head. "My *God*, Carol. God, I feel good, you know? I feel better than I have all summer." He lowered his voice. "Come over tonight, will you?"

He reached under the table and put his hand on her knee. She turned red again. She raised her eyes and looked around the dining room. But no one was paying any attention to them. She nodded quickly. Then she reached under the table and touched his hand.

That afternoon he arrived home to find his house neat and orderly and his children in clean clothes. In the kitchen, Keith and Sarah stood on chairs, helping Mrs Webster with gingerbread cookies. Sarah's hair was out of her face and held back with a barrette.

"Daddy!" his children cried, happy, when they saw him.

"Keith, Sarah," he said. "Mrs Webster, I – " But she didn't let him finish.

"We've had a fine day, Mr Carlyle," Mrs Webster said quickly. She wiped her fingers on the apron she was wearing.

It was an old apron with blue windmills on it and it had belonged to Eileen. "Such beautiful children. They're a treasure. Just a treasure."

"I don't know what to say." Carlyle stood by the drainboard and watched Sarah press out some dough. He could smell the spice. He took off his coat and sat down at the kitchen table. He loosened his tie.

"Today was a get-acquainted day," Mrs Webster said. "Tomorrow we have some other plans. I thought we'd walk to the park. We ought to take advantage of this good weather."

"That's a fine idea," Carlyle said. "That's just fine. Good. Good for you, Mrs Webster."

"I'll finish putting these cookies in the oven, and by that time Mr Webster should be here. You said four o'clock? I told him to come at four."

Carlyle nodded, his heart full.

"You had a call today," she said as she went over to the sink with the mixing bowl. "Mrs Carlyle called."

"Mrs Carlyle," he said. He waited for whatever it was Mrs Webster might say next.

"Yes. I identified myself, but she didn't seem surprised to find me here. She said a few words to each of the children."

Carlyle glanced at Keith and Sarah, but they weren't paying any attention. They were lining up cookies on another baking sheet.

Mrs Webster continued. "She left a message. Let me see, I wrote it down, but I think I can remember it. She said, 'Tell him' – that is, tell you – 'what goes around, comes around.' I think that's right. She said you'd understand."

Carlyle stared at her. He heard Mr Webster's truck outside.

"That's Mr Webster," she said and took off the apron.

Carlyle nodded.

"Seven o'clock in the morning?" she asked.

"That will be fine," he said. "And thank you again."

That evening he bathed each of the children, got them into their pyjamas, and then read to them. He listened to their prayers, tucked in their covers, and turned out the light. It was nearly nine o'clock. He made himself a drink and watched something on TV until he heard Carol's car pull into the drive.

Around ten, while they were in bed together, the phone rang. He swore, but he didn't get up to answer it. It kept ringing.

"It might be important," Carol said, sitting up. "It might be my sitter. She has this number."

"It's my wife," Carlyle said. "I know it's her. She's losing her mind. She's going crazy. I'm not going to answer it."

"I have to go pretty soon anyway," Carol said. "It was real sweet tonight, honey." She touched his face.

It was the middle of the fall term. Mrs Webster had been with him for nearly six weeks. During this time, Carlyle's life had undergone a number of changes. For one thing, he was becoming reconciled to the fact that Eileen was gone and, as far as he could understand it, had no intention of coming back. He had stopped imagining that this might change. It was only late at night, on the nights he was not with Carol, that he wished for an end to the love he still had for Eileen and felt tormented as to why all of this had happened. But for the most part he and the children were happy; they thrived under Mrs Webster's attentions. Lately, she'd gotten into the routine of making their dinner and keeping it in the oven, warming, until his arrival home from school. He'd walk in the door to the smell of something good coming from the kitchen and find Keith and Sarah helping to set the dining-room table. Now and again he asked Mrs Webster if she would care for overtime work on Saturdays. She agreed, as long as it wouldn't entail her being at his house before noon. Saturday mornings, she said, she had things to do for Mr Webster and herself. On these days, Carol would leave Dodge with Carlyle's children, all of them under Mrs Webster's care, and Carol and he would drive to a restaurant out in the country for dinner. He believed his life was beginning again. Though he hadn't heard from Eileen since that call six weeks ago, he found himself able to think about her now without either being angry or else feeling close to tears.

At school, they were just leaving the medieval period and about to enter the Gothic. The Renaissance was still some time off, at least not until after the Christmas recess. It was during this time that Carlyle got sick. Overnight, it seemed, his chest tightened and his head began to hurt The joints of his body became stiff. He felt dizzy when he moved around. The headache got worse. He woke up with it on a Sunday and thought of calling Mrs Webster to ask her to come and take the children somewhere. They'd been sweet to him, bringing him glasses of juice and some soda pop. But he couldn't take care of them. On the second morning of his illness, he was just able to get to the phone to call in sick. He gave his name, his school, department, and the nature of his illness to the person who answered the number. Then he recommended Mel Fisher as his substitute. Fisher was a man who painted abstract oils three or four days a week, sixteen hours a day, but who didn't sell or even show his work. He was a friend of Carlyle's. "Get Mel Fisher," Carlyle told the woman on the other end of the line. "Fisher," he whispered.

He made it back to his bed, got under the covers, and went to sleep. In his sleep, he heard the pickup engine running outside, and then the backfire it made as the engine was turned off. Sometime later he heard Mrs Webster's voice outside the bedroom door.

"Mr Carlyle?"

"Yes, Mrs Webster." His voice sounded strange to him. He kept his eyes shut. "I'm sick today. I called the school. I'm going to stay in bed today."

"I see. Don't worry, then," she said. "I'll look after things at this end."

He shut his eyes. Directly, still in a state between sleeping and waking, he thought he heard his front door open and close. He listened. Out in the kitchen, he heard a man say something in a low voice, and a chair being pulled away from the table. Pretty soon he heard the voices of the children. Sometime later – he wasn't sure how much time had passed – he heard Mrs Webster outside his door.

"Mr Carlyle, should I call the doctor?"

"No, that's all right," he said. "I think it's just a bad cold. But I feel hot all over. I think I have too many covers. And it's too warm in the house. Maybe you'll turn down the furnace." Then he felt himself drift back into sleep.

In a little while, he heard the children talking to Mrs Webster in the living room. Were they coming inside or going out? Carlyle wondered. Could it be the next day already?

He went back to sleep. But then he was aware of his door opening. Mrs Webster appeared beside his bed. She put her hand on his forehead.

"You're burning up," she said. "You have a fever."

"I'll be all right," Carlyle said. "I just need to sleep a little longer. And maybe you could turn the furnace down. Please, I'd appreciate it if you could get me some aspirin. I have an awful headache."

Mrs Webster left the room. But his door stood open. Carlyle could hear the TV going out there. "Keep it down, Jim," he heard her say, and the volume was lowered at once. Carlyle fell asleep again.

But he couldn't have slept more than a minute, because Mrs Webster was suddenly back in his room with a tray. She sat down on the side of his bed. He roused himself and tried to sit up. She put a pillow behind his back.

"Take these," she said and gave him some tablets. "Drink this." She held a glass of juice for him. "I also brought you some Cream of Wheat. I want you to eat it. It'll be good for you."

He took the aspirin and drank the juice. He nodded. But he shut his eyes once more. He was going back to sleep.

"Mr Carlyle," she said.

He opened his eyes. "I'm awake," he said. "I'm sorry." He sat up a little. "I'm too warm, that's all. What time is it? Is it eight-thirty yet?"

"It's a little after nine-thirty," she said.

"Nine-thirty," he said.

"Now I'm going to feed this cereal to you. And you're going to open up and eat it. Six bites, that's all. Here, here's the first bite. Open," she said. "You're going to feel better after you eat this. Then I'll let you go back to sleep. You eat this, and then you can sleep all you want."

He ate the cereal she spooned to him and asked for more juice. He drank the juice, and then he pulled down in the bed again. Just as he was going off to sleep, he felt her covering him with another blanket.

The next time he awoke, it was afternoon. He could tell it was afternoon by the pale light that came through his window. He reached up and pulled the curtain back. He could see that it was overcast outside; the wintry sun was behind the clouds. He got out of bed slowly, found his slippers, and put on his robe. He went into the bathroom and looked at himself in the mirror. Then he washed his face and took some more aspirin. He used the towel and then went out to the living room.

On the dining-room table, Mrs Webster had spread some newspaper, and she and the children were pinching clay figures together. They had already made some things that had long necks and bulging eyes, things that resembled giraffes, or else dinosaurs. Mrs Webster looked up as he walked by the table.

"How are you feeling?" Mrs Webster asked him as he settled onto the sofa. He could see into the dining-room area, where Mrs Webster and the children sat at the table.

"Better, thanks. A little better," he said. "I still have a headache, and I feel a little warm." He brought the back of his hand up to his forehead. "But I'm better. Yes, I'm better. Thanks for your help this morning."

"Can I get you anything now?" Mrs Webster said. "Some more juice or some tea? I don't think coffee would hurt, but I think tea would be better. Some juice would be best of all."

"No, no thanks," he said. "I'll just sit here for a while. It's good to be out of bed. I feel a little weak is all. Mrs Webster?"

She looked at him and waited.

"Did I hear Mr Webster in the house this morning? It's fine, of course. I'm just sorry I didn't get a chance to meet him and say hello."

"It was him," she said. "He wanted to meet you, too. I asked him to come in. He just picked the wrong morning, what with you being sick and all. I'd wanted to tell you something about our plans, Mr Webster's and mine, but this morning wasn't a good time for it."

"Tell me what?" he said, alert, fear plucking at his heart.

She shook her head. "It's all right," she said. "It can wait."

"Tell him what?" Sarah said. "Tell him what?"

"What, what?" Keith picked it up. The children stopped what they were doing.

"Just a minute, you two," Mrs Webster said as she got to her feet.

"Mrs Webster, Mrs Webster!" Keith cried.

"Now see here, little man," Mrs Webster said. "I need to talk to your father. Your father is sick today. You just take it easy. You go on and play with your clay. If you don't watch it, your sister is going to get ahead of you with these creatures."

Just as she began to move toward the living room, the phone rang. Carlyle reached over to the end table and picked up the receiver.

As before, he heard faint singing in the wire and knew that it was Eileen. "Yes," he said. "What is it?"

"Carlyle," his wife said, "I know, don't ask me how, that things are not going so well right now. You're sick, aren't you? Richard's been sick, too. It's something going around. He can't keep anything on his stomach. He's already missed a week of rehearsal for this play he's doing. I've had to go down myself and help block out scenes with his assistant. But I didn't call to tell you that. Tell me how things are out there."

"Nothing to tell," Carlyle said. "I'm sick, that's all. A touch of the flu. But I'm getting better."

"Are you still writing in your journal?" she asked. It caught him by surprise. Several years before, he'd told her that he was keeping a journal. Not a diary, he'd said, a journal – as if that explained something. But he'd never shown it to her, and he hadn't written in it for over a year. He'd forgotten about it.

"Because," she said, "you ought to write something in the journal during this period. How you feel and what you're thinking. You know, where your head is at during this period of sickness. Remember, sickness is a message about your health and your well-being. It's telling you things. Keep a record. You know what I mean? When you're well, you can look back and see what the message was. You can read it later, after the fact. Colette did that," Eileen said. "When she had a fever this one time."

"Who?" Carlyle said. "What did you say?"

"Colette," Eileen answered. "The French writer. You know who I'm talking about. We had a book of hers around the house. *Gigi* or something. I didn't read *that* book, but I've been reading her since I've been out here. Richard turned me on to her. She wrote a little book about what it was like, about what she was thinking and feeling the whole time she had this fever. Sometimes her temperature was a hundred and two. Sometimes it was lower. Maybe it went higher than a hundred and two. But a hundred and two was the highest she ever took her temperature and wrote, too, when she had the fever. Anyway, she wrote about it. That's what I'm saying. Try writing about what it's like. Something might come of it," Eileen said and, inexplicably, it seemed to Carlyle, she laughed. "At least later on you'd have an hour-by-hour account of your sickness. To look back at. At least you'd have that to show for it. Right now you've just got this discomfort. You've got to translate that into something usable."

He pressed his fingertips against his temple and shut his eyes. But she was still on the line, waiting for him to say something. What could he say? It was clear to him that she was insane.

"Jesus," he said. "Jesus, Eileen. I don't know what to say

to that. I really don't. I have to go now. Thanks for calling," he said.

"It's all right," she said. "We have to be able to communicate. Kiss the kids for me. Tell them I love them. And Richard sends his hellos to you. Even though he's flat on his back."

"Goodbye," Carlyle said and hung up. Then he brought his hands to his face. He remembered, for some reason, seeing the fat girl make the same gesture that time as she moved toward the car. He lowered his hands and looked at Mrs Webster, who was watching him.

"Not bad news, I hope," she said. The old woman had moved a chair near to where he sat on the sofa.

Carlyle shook his head.

"Good," Mrs Webster said. "That's good. Now, Mr Carlyle, this may not be the best time in the world to talk about this." She glanced out to the dining room. At the table, the children had their heads bent over the clay. "But since it has to be talked about sometime soon, and since it concerns you and the children, and you're up now, I have something to tell you. Jim and I, we're getting on. The thing is, we need something more than we have at the present. Do you know what I'm saying? This is hard for me," she said and shook her head. Carlyle nodded slowly. He knew that she was going to tell him she had to leave. He wiped his face on his sleeve. "Jim's son by a former marriage, Bob – the man is forty years old – called yesterday to invite us to go out to Oregon and help him with his mink ranch. Jim would be doing whatever they do with minks, and I'd cook, buy the groceries, clean house, and do anything else that needed doing. It's a chance for both of us. And it's board and room and then some. Jim and I won't have to worry anymore about what's going to happen to us. You know what I'm saying. Right now, Jim doesn't have anything," she said. "He was sixty-two last week. He hasn't had anything for some time. He came in this morning to tell you about it himself, because I was going to have to give notice, you see. We thought — *I* thought — it would help if Jim was here when I told you." She waited for Carlyle to say something. When he didn't, she went on. "I'll finish out the week, and I could stay on a couple of days next week, if need be. But then, you know, for sure, we really have to leave, and you'll have to wish us luck. I mean, can you imagine — all the way out there to Oregon in that old rattle-trap of ours? But I'm going to miss these little kids. They're so precious."

After a time, when he still hadn't moved to answer her, she got up from her chair and went to sit on the cushion next to his. She touched the sleeve of his robe. "Mr Carlyle?"

"I understand," he said. "I want you to know your being here has made a big difference to me and the children." His head ached so much that he had to squint his eyes. "This headache," he said. "This headache is killing me."

Mrs Webster reached over and laid the back of her hand against his forehead. "You still have some fever," she told him. "I'll get more aspirin. That'll help bring it down. I'm still on the case here," she said. "I'm still the doctor."

"My wife thinks I should write down what this feels like," Carlyle said. "She thinks it might be a good idea to describe what the fever is like. So I can look back later and get the message." He laughed. Some tears came to his eyes. He wiped them away with the heel of his hand.

"I think I'll get your aspirin and juice and then go out there with the kids," Mrs Webster said. "Looks to me like they've about worn out their interest with that clay."

Carlyle was afraid she'd move into the other room and leave him alone. He wanted to talk to her. He cleared his throat. "Mrs Webster, there's something I want you to know. For a long time, my wife and I loved each other more than anything or anybody in the world. And that includes those children. We thought, well, we *knew* that we'd grow old together. And we knew we'd do all the things in the world that we wanted to do, and do them together." He shook his head. That seemed the saddest thing of all to him now – that whatever they did from now on, each would do it without the other.

"There, it's all right," Mrs Webster said. She patted his hand. He sat forward and began to talk again. After a time, the children came out to the living room. Mrs Webster caught their attention and held a finger to her lips. Carlyle looked at them and went on talking. Let them listen, he thought. It concerns them, too. The children seemed to understand they had to remain quiet, even pretend some interest, so they sat down next to Mrs Webster's legs. Then they got down on their stomachs on the carpet and started to giggle. But Mrs Webster looked sternly in their direction, and that stopped it.

Carlyle went on talking. At first, his head still ached, and he felt awkward to be in his pyjamas on the sofa with this old woman beside him, waiting patiently for him to go on to the next thing. But then his headache went away. And soon he stopped feeling awkward and forgot how he was supposed to feel. He had begun his story somewhere in the middle, after the children were born. But then he backed up and started at the beginning, back when Eileen was eighteen and he was nineteen, a boy and girl in love, burning with it.

He stopped to wipe his forehead. He moistened his lips.

"Go on," Mrs Webster said. "I know what you're saying. You just keep talking, Mr Carlyle. Sometimes it's good to talk about it. Sometimes it has to be talked about. Besides,

I want to hear it. And you're going to feel better afterwards. Something just like it happened to me once, something like what you're describing. Love. That's what it is."

The children fell asleep on the carpet. Keith had his thumb in his mouth. Carlyle was still talking when Mr Webster came to the door, knocked, and then stepped inside to collect Mrs Webster.

"Sit down, Jim," Mrs Webster said. "There's no hurry. Go on with what you were saying, Mr Carlyle."

Carlyle nodded at the old man, and the old man nodded back, then got himself one of the dining-room chairs and carried it into the living room. He brought the chair close to the sofa and sat down on it with a sigh. Then he took off his cap and wearily lifted one leg over the other. When Carlyle began talking again, the old man put both feet on the floor. The children woke up. They sat up on the carpet and rolled their heads back and forth. But by then Carlyle had said all he knew to say, so he stopped talking.

"Good. Good for you," Mrs Webster said when she saw he had finished. "You're made out of good stuff. And so is she — so is Mrs Carlyle. And don't you forget it. You're both going to be okay after this is over." She got up and took off the apron she'd been wearing. Mr Webster got up, too, and put his cap back on.

At the door, Carlyle shook hands with both of the Websters.

"So long," Jim Webster said. He touched the bill of his cap.

"Good luck to you," Carlyle said.

Mrs Webster said she'd see him in the morning then, bright and early as always.

As if something important had been settled, Carlyle said, "Right!"

The old couple went carefully along the walk and got into

their truck. Jim Webster bent down under the dashboard. Mrs Webster looked at Carlyle and waved. It was then, as he stood at the window, that he felt something come to an end. It had to do with Eileen and the life before this. Had he ever waved at her? He must have, of course, he knew he had, yet he could not remember just now. But he understood it was over, and he felt able to let her go. He was sure their life together had happened in the way he said it had. But it was something that had passed. And that passing – though it had seemed impossible and he'd fought against it – would become a part of him now, too, as surely as anything else he'd left behind.

As the pickup lurched forward, he lifted his arm once more. He saw the old couple lean toward him briefly as they drove away. Then he brought his arm down and turned to his children.

The Bridle

This old station wagon with Minnesota plates pulls into a parking space in front of the window. There's a man and woman in the front seat, two boys in the back. It's July, temperature's one hundred plus. These people look whipped. There are clothes hanging inside; suitcases, boxes, and such piled in back. From what Harley and I put together later, that's all they had left after the bank in Minnesota took their house, their pickup, their tractor, the farm implements, and a few cows.

The people inside sit for a minute, as if collecting themselves. The air-conditioner in our apartment is going full blast. Harley's around in back cutting grass. There's some discussion in the front seat, and then she and him get out and start for the front door. I pat my hair to make sure that it's in place and wait till they push the doorbell for the second time. Then I go to let them in. "You're looking for an apartment?" I say. "Come on in here where it's cool." I show them into the living room. The living room is where I do business. It's where I collect the rents, write the receipts, and talk to interested parties. I also do hair. I call myself a *stylist*. That's what my cards say. I don't like the word *beautician*. It's an old-time word. I have the chair in a corner of the living room, and a dryer I can pull up to the back of the chair. And there's a sink that Harley put in a few years ago. Alongside the chair, I have a table with some magazines. The magazines are old.

174

The covers are gone from some of them. But people will look at anything while they're under the dryer.

The man says his name.

"My name is Holits."

He tells me she's his wife. But she won't look at me. She looks at her nails instead. She and Holits won't sit down, either. He says they're interested in one of the furnished units.

"How many of you?" But I'm just saying what I always say. I know how many. I saw the two boys in the back seat. Two and two is four.

"Me and her and the boys. The boys are thirteen and fourteen, and they'll share a room, like always."

She has her arms crossed and is holding the sleeves of her blouse. She takes in the chair and the sink as if she's never seen their like before. Maybe she hasn't.

"I do hair," I say.

She nods. Then she gives my prayer plant the once-over. It has exactly five leaves to it.

"That needs watering," I say. I go over and touch one of its leaves. "Everything around here needs water. There's not enough water in the air. It rains three times a year if we're lucky. But you'll get used to it. We had to get used to it. But everything here is air-conditioned."

"How much is the place?" Holits wants to know.

I tell him and he turns to her to see what she thinks. But he may as well have been looking at the wall. She won't give him back his look. "I guess we'll have you show us," he says. So I move to get the key for 17, and we go outside.

I hear Harley before I see him.

Then he comes into sight between the buildings. He's moving along behind the power mower in his Bermudas and

T-shirt, wearing the straw hat he bought in Nogales. He spends his time cutting grass and doing the small maintenance work. We work for a corporation, Fulton Terrace, Inc. They own the place. If anything major goes wrong, like air-conditioning trouble or something serious in the plumbing department, we have a list of phone numbers.

I wave. I have to. Harley takes a hand off the mower handle and signals. Then he pulls the hat down over his forehead and gives his attention back to what he's doing. He comes to the end of his cut, makes his turn, and starts back toward the street.

"That's Harley." I have to shout it. We go in at the side of the building and up some stairs. "What kind of work are you in, Mr Holits?" I ask him.

"He's a farmer," she says.

"No more."

"Not much to farm around here." I say it without thinking.

"We had us a farm in Minnesota. Raised wheat. A few cattle. And Holits knows horses. He knows everything there is about horses."

"That's all right, Betty."

I get a piece of the picture then. Holits is unemployed. It's not my affair, and I feel sorry if that's the case — it is, it turns out — but as we stop in front of the unit, I have to say something. "If you decide, it's first month, last month, and one-fifty as security deposit." I look down at the pool as I say it. Some people are sitting in deck chairs, and there's somebody in the water.

Holits wipes his face with the back of his hand. Harley's mower is clacking away. Farther off, cars speed by on Calle Verde. The two boys have got out of the station wagon. One of them is standing at military attention, legs together, arms at his sides. But as I watch, I see him begin to flap his arms up and down and jump, like he intends to take off and fly. The other one is squatting down on the driver's side of the station wagon, doing knee bends.

I turn to Holits.

"Let's have a look," he says.

I turn the key and the door opens. It's just a little two-bedroom furnished apartment. Everybody has seen dozens. Holits stops in the bathroom long enough to flush the toilet. He watches till the tank fills. Later, he says, "This could be our room." He's talking about the bedroom that looks out over the pool. In the kitchen, the woman takes hold of the edge of the drainboard and stares out the window.

"That's the swimming pool," I say.

She nods. "We stayed in some motels that had swimming pools. But in one pool they had too much chlorine in the water."

I wait for her to go on. But that's all she says. I can't think of anything else, either.

"I guess we won't waste any more time. I guess we'll take it." Holits looks at her as he says it. This time she meets his eyes. She nods. He lets out breath through his teeth. Then she does something. She begins snapping her fingers. One hand is still holding the edge of the drainboard, but with her other hand she begins snapping her fingers. Snap, snap, snap, like she was calling her dog, or else trying to get somebody's attention. Then she stops and runs her nails across the counter.

I don't know what to make of it. Holits doesn't either. He moves his feet.

"We'll walk back to the office and make things official," I say. "I'm glad."

I *was* glad. We had a lot of empty units for this time of year. And these people seemed like dependable people.

Down on their luck, that's all. No disgrace can be attached to that.

Holits pays in cash – first, last, and the one-fifty deposit. He counts out bills of fifty-dollar denomination while I watch. US Grants, Harley calls them, though he's never seen many. I write out the receipt and give him two keys. "You're all set."

He looks at the keys. He hands her one. "So, we're in Arizona. Never thought you'd see Arizona, did you?"

She shakes her head. She's touching one of the prayer-plant leaves.

"Needs water," I say.

She lets go of the leaf and turns to the window. I go over next to her. Harley is still cutting grass. but he's around in front now. There's been this talk of farming, so for a minute I think of Harley moving along behind a plow instead of behind his Black and Decker power mower.

I watch them unload their boxes, suitcases, and clothes. Holits carries in something that has straps hanging from it. It takes a minute, but then I figure out it's a bridle. I don't know what to do next. I don't feel like doing anything. So I take the Grants out of the cashbox. I just put them in there, but I take them out again. The bills have come from Minnesota. Who knows where they'll be this time next week? They could be in Las Vegas. All I know about Las Vegas is what I see on TV – about enough to put into a thimble. I can imagine one of the Grants finding its way out to Waikiki Beach, or else some other place. Miami or New York City. New Orleans. I think about one of those bills changing hands during Mardi Gras. They could go anyplace, and anything could happen because of them. I write my name in ink across Grant's broad old forehead: MARGE. I print it. I do it on every one. Right over his thick brows. People will stop in the midst of their spending and wonder. Who's this Marge? That's what they'll ask themselves, Who's this Marge?

Harley comes in from outside and washes his hands in my sink. He knows it's something I don't like him to do. But he goes ahead and does it anyway.

"Those people from Minnesota," he says. "The Swedes. They're a long way from home." He dries his hands on a paper towel. He wants me to tell him what I know. But I don't know anything. They don't look like Swedes and they don't talk like Swedes.

"They're not Swedes," I tell him. But he acts like he doesn't hear me.

"So what's he do?"

"He's a farmer."

"What do you know about that?"

Harley takes his hat off and puts it on my chair. He runs a hand through his hair. Then he looks at the hat and puts it on again. He may as well be glued to it. "There's not much to farm around here. Did you tell him that?" He gets a can of soda pop from the fridge and goes to sit in his recliner. He picks up the remote-control, pushes something, and the TV sizzles on. He pushes some more buttons until he finds what he's looking for. It's a hospital show. "What else does the Swede do? Besides farm?"

I don't know, so I don't say anything. But Harley's already taken up with his program. He's probably forgotten he asked me the question. A siren goes off. I hear the screech of tires. On the screen, an ambulance has come to a stop in front of an emergency-room entrance, its red lights flashing. A man jumps out and runs around to open up the back.

The next afternoon the boys borrow the hose and wash the station wagon. They clean the outside and the inside. A little later I notice her drive away. She's wearing high heels and a nice dress. Hunting up a job, I'd say. After a while, I see the boys messing around the pool in their bathing suits. One of them springs off the board and swims all the way to the other end underwater. He comes up blowing water and shaking his head. The other boy, the one who'd been doing knee bends the day before, lies on his stomach on a towel at the far side of the pool. But this one boy keeps swimming back and forth from one end of the pool to the other, touching the wall and turning back with a little kick.

There are two other people out there. They're in lounge chairs, one on either side of the pool. One of them is Irving Cobb, a cook at Denny's. He calls himself Spuds. People have taken to calling him that, Spuds, instead of Irv or some other nickname. Spuds is fifty-five and bald. He already looks like beef jerky, but he wants more sun. Right now, his new wife, Linda Cobb, is at work at the K Mart. Spuds works nights. But him and Linda Cobb have it arranged so they take their Saturdays and Sundays off. Connie Nova is in the other chair. She's sitting up and rubbing lotion on her legs. She's nearly naked — just this little two-piece suit covering her. Connie Nova is a cocktail waitress. She moved in here six months ago with her so-called fiancé, an alcoholic lawyer. But she got rid of him. Now she lives with a long-haired student from the college whose name is Rick. I happen to know he's away right now, visiting his folks. Spuds and Connie are wearing dark glasses. Connie's portable radio is going.

Spuds was a recent widower when he moved in, a year or so back. But after a few months of being a bachelor again, he got married to Linda. She's a red-haired woman in her thirties. I don't know how they met. But one night a couple of months ago Spuds and the new Mrs Cobb had Harley and me over to a nice dinner that Spuds fixed. After dinner, we sat in their living room drinking sweet drinks out of big glasses. Spuds asked if we wanted to see home movies. We said sure. So Spuds set up his screen and his projector. Linda Cobb poured us more of that sweet drink. Where's the harm? I asked myself. Spuds began to show films of a trip he and his dead wife had made to Alaska. It began with her getting on the plane in Seattle. Spuds talked as he ran the projector. The deceased was in her fifties, good-looking, though maybe a little heavy. Her hair was nice.

"That's Spuds's first wife," Linda Cobb said. "That's the first Mrs Cobb."

"That's Evelyn," Spuds said.

The first wife stayed on the screen for a long time. It was funny seeing her and hearing them talk about her like that. Harley passed me a look, so I know he was thinking something, too. Linda Cobb asked if we wanted another drink or a macaroon. We didn't. Spuds was saying something about the first Mrs Cobb again. She was still at the entrance to the plane, smiling and moving her mouth even if all you could hear was the film going through the projector. People had to go around her to get on the plane. She kept waving at the camera, waving at us there in Spuds's living room. She waved and waved. "There's Evelyn again," the new Mrs Cobb would say each time the first Mrs Cobb appeared on the screen.

Spuds would have shown films all night, but we said we had to go. Harley made the excuse.

I don't remember what he said.

Connie Nova is lying on her back in the chair, dark glasses covering half of her face. Her legs and stomach shine with oil. One night, not long after she moved in, she had a party.

This was before she kicked the lawyer out and took up with the long-hair. She called her party a housewarming. Harley and I were invited, along with a bunch of other people. We went, but we didn't care for the company. We found a place to sit close to the door, and that's where we stayed till we left. It wasn't all that long, either. Connie's boyfriend was giving a door prize. It was the offer of his legal services, without charge, for the handling of a divorce. Anybody's divorce. Anybody who wanted to could draw a card out of the bowl he was passing around. When the bowl came our way, everybody began to laugh. Harley and I swapped glances. I didn't draw. Harley didn't draw, either. But I saw him look in the bowl at the pile of cards. Then he shook his head and handed the bowl to the person next to him. Even Spuds and the new Mrs Cobb drew cards. The winning card had something written across the back. "Entitles bearer to one free uncontested divorce," and the lawyer's signature and the date. The lawyer was a drunk, but I say this is no way to conduct your life. Everybody but us had put his hand into the bowl, like it was a fun thing to do. The woman who drew the winning card clapped. It was like one of those game shows. "Goddamn, this is the first time I ever won anything!" I was told she had a husband in the military. There's no way of knowing if she still has him, or if she got her divorce, because Connie Nova took up with a different set of friends after she and the lawyer went their separate ways.

We left the party right after the drawing. It made such an impression we couldn't say much, except one of us said, "I don't believe I saw what I think I saw."

Maybe I said it.

A week later Harley asks if the Swede — he means Holits — has found work yet. We've just had lunch, and Harley's in his chair with his can of pop. But he hasn't turned his TV on. I say I don't know. And I don't. I wait to see what else he has to say. But he doesn't say anything else. He shakes his head. He seems to think about something. Then he pushes a button and the TV comes to life.

She finds a job. She starts working as a waitress in an Italian restaurant a few blocks from here. She works a split shift, doing lunches and then going home, then back to work again in time for the dinner shift. She's meeting herself coming and going. The boys swim all day, while Holits stays inside the apartment. I don't know what he does in there. Once, I did her hair and she told me a few things. She told me she did waitressing when she was just out of high school and that's where she met Holits. She served him some pancakes in a place back in Minnesota.

She'd walked down that morning and asked me could I do her a favor. She wanted me to fix her hair after her lunch shift and have her out in time for her dinner shift. Could I do it? I told her I'd check the book. I asked her to step inside. It must have been a hundred degrees already.

"I know it's short notice," she said. "But when I came in from work last night, I looked in the mirror and saw my roots showing. I said to myself, 'I need a treatment.' I don't know where else to go."

I find Friday, August 14. There's nothing on the page.

"I could work you in at two-thirty, or else at three o'clock," I say.

"Three would be better," she says. "I have to run for it now before I'm late. I work for a real bastard. See you later."

At two-thirty, I tell Harley I have a customer, so he'll have to take his baseball game into the bedroom. He grumps, but he winds up the cord and wheels the set out back. He closes the door. I make sure everything I need is ready. I fix up the magazines so they're easy to get to. Then I sit next to the dryer and file my nails. I'm wearing the rose-colored uniform that I put on when I do hair. I go on filing my nails and looking up at the window from time to time.

She walks by the window and then pushes the doorbell. "Come on in," I call. "It's unlocked."

She's wearing the black-and-white uniform from her job. I can see how we're both wearing uniforms. "Sit down, honey, and we'll get started." She looks at the nail file. "I give manicures, too," I say.

She settles into the chair and draws a breath.

I say, "Put your head back. That's it. Close your eyes now, why don't you? Just relax. First I'll shampoo you and touch up these roots here. Then we'll go from there. How much time do you have?"

"I have to be back there at five-thirty."

"We'll get you fixed up."

"I can eat at work. But I don't know what Holits and the boys will do for their supper."

"They'll get along fine without you."

I start the warm water and then notice Harley's left me some dirt and grass. I wipe up his mess and start over.

I say, "If they want, they can just walk down the street to the hamburger place. It won't hurt them."

"They won't do that. Anyway, I don't want them to have to go there."

It's none of my business, so I don't say any more. I make up a nice lather and go to work. After I've done the shampoo, rinse, and set, I put her under the dryer. Her eyes have closed. I think she could be asleep. So I take one of her hands and begin.

"No manicure." She opens her eyes and pulls away her hand.

'It's all right, honey. The first manicure is always no charge."

She gives me back her hand and picks up one of the magazines and rests it in her lap. "They're his boys," she says. "From his first marriage. He was divorced when we met. But I love them like they were my own. I couldn't love them any more if I tried. Not even if I was their natural mother."

I turn the dryer down a notch so that it's making a low, quiet sound. I keep on with her nails. Her hand starts to relax.

"She lit out on them, on Holits and the boys, on New Year's Day ten years ago. They never heard from her again." I can see she wants to tell me about it. And that's fine with me. They like to talk when they're in the chair. I go on using the file. "Holits got the divorce. Then he and I started going out. Then we got married. For a long time, we had us a life. It had its ups and downs. But we thought we were working toward something." She shakes her head. "But something happened. Something happened to Holits, I mean. One thing happened was he got interested in horses. This one particular race horse, he bought it, you know – something down, something each month. He took it around to the tracks. He was still up before daylight, like always, still doing the chores and such. I thought everything was all right. But I don't know anything. If you want the truth, I'm not so good at waiting tables. I think those wops would fire me at the drop of a hat, if I gave them a reason. Or for no reason. What if I got fired? Then what?"

I say, "Don't worry, honey. They're not going to fire you."

Pretty soon she picks up another magazine. But she doesn't open it. She just holds it and goes on talking. "Anyway, there's this horse of his. Fast Betty. The Betty part is a joke. But he says it can't help but be a winner if he names it after me. A big winner, all right. The fact is, wherever it ran, it lost. Every race. Betty Longshot – that's what it should have been called. In the beginning, I went to a few races. But the horse always ran ninety-nine to one. Odds like that. But Holits is stubborn if he's anything. He wouldn't give up. He'd bet on the horse and bet on the horse. Twenty dollars to win. Fifty dollars to win. Plus all the other things it costs for keeping a horse. I know it don't sound like a large amount. But it adds up. And when the odds were like that – ninety-nine to one, you know – sometimes he'd buy a combination ticket. He'd ask me if I realized how much money we'd make if the horse came in. But it didn't, and I quit going."

I keep on with what I'm doing. I concentrate on her nails. "You have nice cuticles," I say. "Look here at your cuticles. See these little half-moons? Means your blood's good."

She brings her hand up close and looks. "What do you know about that?" She shrugs. She lets me take her hand again. She's still got things to tell. "Once, when I was in high school, a counselor asked me to come to her office. She did it with all the girls, one of us at a time. 'What dreams do you have?' this woman asked me. 'What do you see yourself doing in ten years? Twenty years?' I was sixteen or seventeen. I was just a kid. I couldn't think what to answer. I just sat there like a lump. This counselor was about the age I am now. I thought she was *old*. She's old, I said to myself. I knew *her* life was half over. And I felt like I knew something she didn't. Something she'd never know. A secret. Something nobody's supposed to know, or ever talk about. So I stayed quiet. I just shook my head. She must've written me off as a dope. But I couldn't say anything. You know what I mean? I thought I knew things she couldn't guess at. Now, if anybody asked me that question again, about my dreams and all, I'd tell them."

"What would you tell them, honey?" I have her other hand now. But I'm not doing her nails. I'm just holding it, waiting to hear.

She moves forward in the chair. She tries to take her hand back.

"What would you tell them?"

She sighs and leans back. She lets me keep the hand. "I'd say, 'Dreams, you know, are what you wake up from.' That's what I'd say." She smooths the lap of her skirt. "If anybody asked, that's what I'd say. But they won't ask." She lets out her breath again. "So how much longer?" she says.

"Not long," I say.

"You don't know what it's like."

"Yes, I do," I say. I pull the stool right up next to her legs. I'm starting to tell how it was before we moved here, and how it's still like that. But Harley picks right then to come out of the bedroom. He doesn't look at us. I hear the TV jabbering away in the bedroom. He goes to the sink and draws a glass of water. He tips his head back to drink. His Adam's apple moves up and down in his throat.

I move the dryer away and touch the hair at both sides of her head. I lift one of the curls just a little.

I say, "You look brand-new, honey."

"Don't I wish."

The boys keep on swimming all day, every day, till their school starts. Betty keeps on at her job. But for some reason she doesn't come back to get her hair done. I don't know why this is. Maybe she doesn't think I did a good job. Sometimes I lie awake, Harley sleeping like a grindstone beside me, and try to picture myself in Betty's shoes. I wonder what I'd do then.

Holits sends one of his sons with the rent on the first of September, and on the first of October, too. He still pays in cash. I take the money from the boy, count the bills right there in front of him, and then write out the receipt. Holits has found work of some sort. I think so, anyway. He drives off every day with the station wagon. I see him leave early in the morning and drive back late in the afternoon. She goes past the window at ten-thirty and comes back at three. If she sees me, she gives me a little wave. But she's not smiling. Then I see Betty again at five, walking back to the restaurant. Holits drives in a little later. This goes on till the middle of October.

Meanwhile, the Holits couple acquainted themselves with Connie Nova and her long-hair friend, Rick. And they also met up with Spuds and the new Mrs Cobb. Sometimes, on a Sunday afternoon, I'd see all of them sitting around the pool, drinks in their hands, listening to Connie's portable radio. One time Harley said he saw them all behind the building, in the barbecue area. They were in their bathing suits then, too. Harley said the Swede had a chest like a bull. Harley said they were eating hot dogs and drinking whiskey. He said they were drunk.

It was Saturday, and it was after eleven at night. Harley was asleep in his chair. Pretty soon I'd have to get up and turn off the set. When I did that, I knew he'd wake up. "Why'd you turn it off? I was watching that show." That's what he'd say. That's what he always said. Anyway, the TV was going, I had the curlers in, and there's a magazine on my lap. Now and then I'd look up. But I couldn't get settled on the show. They were all out there in the pool area — Spuds and Linda Cobb, Connie Nova and the long-hair, Holits and Betty. We have a rule against anyone being out there after ten. But this night they didn't care about rules. If Harley woke up, he'd go out and say something. I felt it was all right for them to have their fun, but it was time for it to stop. I kept getting up and going over to the window. All of them except Betty had on bathing suits. She was still in her uniform. But she had her shoes off, a glass in her hand, and she was drinking right along with the rest of them. I kept putting off having to turn off the set. Then one of them shouted something, and another one took it up and began to laugh. I looked and saw Holits finish off his drink. He put the glass down on the deck. Then he walked over to the cabana. He dragged up one of the tables and climbed onto that. Then – he seemed to do it without any effort at all – he lifted up onto the roof of the cabana. It's true, I thought; he's strong. The long-hair claps his hands, like he's all for this. The rest of them are hooting Holits on, too. I know I'm going to have to go out there and put a stop to it.

Harley's slumped in his chair. The TV's still going. I ease the door open, step out, and then push it shut behind me. Holits is up on the roof of the cabana. They're egging him on. They're saying, "Go on, you can do it." "Don't bellyflop, now." "I double-dare you." Things like that.

Then I hear Betty's voice. "Holits, think what you're doing." But Holits just stands there at the edge. He looks down at the water. He seems to be figuring how much of a run he's going to have to make to get out there. He backs up to the far side. He spits in his palm and rubs his hands together. Spuds calls out, "That's it, boy! You'll do it now."

I see him hit the deck. I hear him, too.

"Holits!" Betty cries.

They all hurry over to him. By the time I get there, he's sitting up. Rick is holding him by the shoulders and yelling into his face. "Holits! Hey, man!"

Holits has this gash on his forehead, and his eyes are glassy. Spuds and Rick help him into a chair. Somebody gives him a towel. But Holits holds the towel like he doesn't know what he's supposed to do with it. Somebody else hands him a drink. But Holits doesn't know what to do with that, either. People keep saying things to him. Holits brings the towel up to his face. Then he takes it away and looks at the blood. But he just looks at it. He can't seem to understand anything.

"Let me see him." I get around in front of him. It's bad. "Holits, are you all right?" But Holits just looks at me, and then his eyes drift off. "I think he'd best go to the emergency room." Betty looks at me when I say this and begins to shake her head. She looks back at Holits. She gives him another towel. I think she's sober. But the rest of them are drunk. Drunk is the best that can be said for them.

Spuds picks up what I said. "Let's take him to the emergency room."

Rick says, "I'll go, too."

"We'll all go," Connie Nova says.

"We better stick together," Linda Cobb says.

"Holits." I say his name again.

"I can't go it," Holits says.

"What'd he say?" Connie Nova asks me.

"He said he can't go it," I tell her.

"Go what? What's he talking about?" Rick wants to know.

"Say again?" Spuds says. "I didn't hear."

"He says he can't go it. I don't think he knows what he's talking about. You'd best take him to the hospital," I say. Then I remember Harley and the rules. "You shouldn't have been out here. Any of you. We have rules. Now go on and take him to the hospital."

"Let's take him to the hospital," Spuds says like it's something he's just thought of. He might be farther gone than any of them. For one thing, he can't stand still. He weaves. And he keeps picking up his feet and putting them down again. The hair on his chest is snow white under the overhead pool lights.

"I'll get the car." That's what the long-hair says. "Connie, let me have the keys."

"I can't go it," Holits says. The towel has moved down to his chin. But the cut is on his forehead.

"Get him that terry-cloth robe. He can't go to the hospital that way." Linda Cobb says that. "Holits! Holits, it's us." She waits and then she takes the glass of whiskey from Holits's fingers and drinks from it.

I can see people at some of the windows, looking down on the commotion. Lights are going on. "Go to bed!" someone yells.

Finally, the long-hair brings Connie's Datsun from behind the building and drives it up close to the pool. The head-lights are on bright. He races the engine.

"For Christ's sake, go to bed!" the same person yells. More people come to their windows. I expect to see Harley come out any minute, wearing his hat, steaming. Then I think, No, he'll sleep through it. Just forget Harley.

Spuds and Connie Nova get on either side of Holits. Holits can't walk straight. He's wobbly. Part of it's because he's drunk. But there's no question he's hurt himself. They get him into the car, and they all crowd inside, too. Betty is the last to get in. She has to sit on somebody's lap. Then they drive off. Whoever it was that has been yelling slams the window shut.

The whole next week Holits doesn't leave the place. And I think Betty must have quit her job, because I don't see her pass the window anymore. When I see the boys go by, I step outside and ask them, point-blank: "How's your dad?"

"He hurt his head," one of them says.

I wait in hopes they'll say some more. But they don't. They shrug and go on to school with their lunch sacks and binders. Later, I was sorry I hadn't asked after their step-mom.

When I see Holits outside, wearing a bandage and standing on his balcony, he doesn't even nod. He acts like I'm a stranger. It's like he doesn't know me or doesn't want to know me. Harley says he's getting the same treatment. He doesn't like it. "What's with him?" Harley wants to know. "Damn Swede. What happened to his head? Somebody belt him or what?" I don't tell Harley anything when he says that. I don't go into it at all.

Then that Sunday afternoon I see one of the boys carry out a box and put it in the station wagon. He goes back upstairs. But pretty soon he comes back down with another box, and he puts that in, too. It's then I know they're making ready to leave. But I don't say what I know to Harley. He'll know everything soon enough.

Next morning, Betty sends one of the boys down. He's got a note that says she's sorry but they have to move. She gives me her sister's address in Indio where she says we can send the deposit to. She points out they're leaving eight days before their rent is up. She hopes there might be something in the way of a refund there, even though they haven't given the thirty days' notice. She says, "Thanks for everything. Thanks for doing my hair that time." She signs the note, "Sincerely, Betty Holits."

"What's your name?" I ask the boy.

"Billy."

"Billy, tell her I said I'm real sorry."

Harley reads what she's written, and he says it will be a cold day in hell before they see any money back from Fulton Terrace. He says he can't understand these people. "People who sail through life like the world owes them a living." He asks me where they're going. But I don't have any idea where they're going. Maybe they're going back to Minnesota. How do I know where going? But I don't think they're going back to Minnesota. I think they're going someplace else to try their luck.

Connie Nova and Spuds have their chairs in the usual places, one on either side of the pool. From time to time, they look over at the Holits boys carrying things out to the station wagon. Then Holits himself comes out with some clothes over his arm. Connie Nova and Spuds holler and wave. Holits looks at them like he doesn't know them. But then he raises up his free hand. Just raises it, that's all. They wave. Then Holits is waving. He keeps waving at them, even after they've stopped. Betty comes downstairs and touches his arm. She doesn't wave. She won't even look at these people. She says something to Holits, and he goes on to the car. Connie Nova lies back in her chair and reaches over to turn up her portable radio. Spuds holds his sunglasses and watches Holits and Betty for a while. Then he fixes the glasses over his ears. He settles himself in the lounge chair and goes back to tanning his leathery old self.

Finally, they're all loaded and ready to move on. The boys are in the back, Holits behind the wheel, Betty in the seat right up next to him. It's just like it was when they drove in here.

"What are you looking at?" Harley says.

He's taking a break. He's in his chair, watching the TV. But he gets up and comes over to the window.

"Well, there they go. They don't know where they're going or what they're going to do. Crazy Swede."

I watch them drive out of the lot and turn onto the road that's going to take them to the freeway. Then I look at

Harley again. He's settling into his chair. He has his can of pop, and he's wearing his straw hat. He acts like nothing has happened or ever will happen.

"Harley?"

But, of course, he can't hear me. I go over and stand in front of his chair. He's surprised. He doesn't know what to make of it. He leans back, just sits there looking at me.

The phone starts ringing.

"Get that, will you?" he says.

I don't answer him. Why should I?

"Then let it ring," he says.

I go find the mop, some rags, SOS pads, and a bucket. The phone stops ringing. He's still sitting in his chair. But he's turned off the TV. I take the passkey, go outside and up the stairs to 17. I let myself in and walk through the living room to their kitchen – what used to be their kitchen.

The counters have been wiped down, the sink and cupboards are clean. It's not so bad. I leave the cleaning things on the stove and go take a look at the bathroom. Nothing there a little steel wool won't take care of. Then I open the door to the bedroom that looks our over the pool. The blinds are raised, the bed is stripped. The floor shines. "Thanks," I say out loud. Wherever she's going, I wish her luck. "Good luck, Betty." One of the bureau drawers is open and I go to close it. Back in a corner of the drawer I see the bridle he was carrying in when he first came. It must have been passed over in their hurry. But maybe it wasn't. Maybe the man left it on purpose.

"Bridle," I say. I hold it up to the window and look at it in the light. It's not fancy, it's just an old dark leather bridle. I don't know much about them. But I know that one part of it fits in the mouth. That part's called the bit. It's made of steel. Reins go over the head and up to where they're held on the neck between the fingers. The rider pulls the reins this way and that, and the horse turns. It's simple. The bit's heavy and cold. If you had to wear this thing between your teeth, I guess you'd catch on in a hurry. When you felt it pull, you'd know it was time. You'd know you were going somewhere.

Cathedral

This blind man, an old friend of my wife's, he was on his way to spend the night. His wife had died. So he was visiting the dead wife's relatives in Connecticut. He called my wife from his in-laws'. Arrangements were made. He would come by train, a five-hour trip, and my wife would meet him at the station. She hadn't seen him since she worked for him one summer in Seattle ten years ago. But she and the blind man had kept in touch. They made tapes and mailed them back and forth. I wasn't enthusiastic about his visit. He was no one I knew. And his being blind bothered me. My idea of blindness came from the movies. In the movies, the blind moved slowly and never laughed. Sometimes they were led by seeing-eye dogs. A blind man in my house was not something I looked forward to.

That summer in Seattle she had needed a job. She didn't have any money. The man she was going to marry at the end of the summer was in officers' training school. He didn't have any money, either. But she was in love with the guy, and he was in love with her, etc. She'd seen something in the paper: HELP WANTED − *Reading to Blind Man*, and a telephone number. She phoned and went over, was hired on the spot. She'd worked with this blind man all summer. She read stuff to him, case studies, reports, that sort of thing. She helped him organize his little office in the county social-service department. They'd become good friends, my wife and the blind man. How do I know these things? She told me. And she told me something else. On her last day in the office, the blind man asked if he could touch her face. She agreed to this. She told me he touched his fingers to every part of her face, her nose – even her neck! She never forgot it. She even tried to write a poem about it. She was always trying to write a poem. She wrote a poem or two every year, usually after something really important had happened to her.

When we first started going out together, she showed me the poem. In the poem, she recalled his fingers and the way they had moved around over her face. In the poem, she talked about what she had felt at the time, about what went through her mind when the blind man touched her nose and lips. I can remember I didn't think much of the poem. Of course, I didn't tell her that. Maybe I just don't understand poetry. I admit it's not the first thing I reach for when I pick up something to read.

Anyway, this man who'd first enjoyed her favors, the officer-to-be, he'd been her childhood sweetheart. So okay. I'm saying that at the end of the summer she let the blind man run his hands over her face, said goodbye to him, married her childhood etc., who was now a commissioned officer, and she moved away from Seattle. But they'd kept in touch, she and the blind man. She made the first contact after a year or so. She called him up one night from an Air Force base in Alabama. She wanted to talk. They talked. He asked her to send him a tape and tell him about her life. She did this. She sent the tape. On the tape, she told the blind man about her husband and about their life together in the military. She told the blind man she loved her husband but she didn't like it where they lived and she didn't like it that he was a part of the military industrial thing. She told the blind man she'd written a poem and he was in it. She told him that she was writing a poem about what it was like to be an Air Force officer's wife. The poem wasn't finished yet. She was still writing it. The blind man made a tape. He sent her the tape. She made a tape. This went on for years. My wife's officer was posted to one base and then another. She sent tapes from Moody AFB, McGuire, McConnell, and finally Travis, near Sacramento, where one night she got to feeling lonely and cut off from people she kept losing in that moving-around life. She got to feeling she couldn't go it another step. She went in and swallowed all the pills and capsules in the medicine chest and washed them down with a bottle of gin. Then she got into a hot bath and passed out.

But instead of dying, she got sick. She threw up. Her officer – why should he have a name? he was the childhood sweetheart, and what more does he want? – came home from somewhere, found her, and called the ambulance. In time, she put it all on a tape and sent the tape to the blind man. Over the years, she put all kinds of stuff on tapes and sent the tapes off lickety-split. Next to writing a poem every year, I think it was her chief means of recreation. On one tape, she told the blind man she'd decided to live away from her officer for a time. On another tape, she told him about her divorce. She and I began going out, and of course she told her blind man about it. She told him everything, or so it seemed to me. Once she asked me if I'd like to hear the latest tape from the blind man. This was a year ago. I was on the tape, she said. So I said okay, I'd listen to it. I got us drinks and we settled down in the living room. We made ready to listen. First she inserted the tape into the player and adjusted a couple of dials. Then she pushed a lever. The tape squeaked and someone began to talk in this loud voice. She lowered the volume. After a few minutes of harmless chitchat, I heard my own name in the mouth of this stranger, this blind man I didn't even know! And then this: "From all you've said about him, I can only conclude –" But we were interrupted, a knock at the door, something, and we didn't ever get back to the tape. Maybe it was just as well. I'd heard all I wanted to.

Now this same blind man was coming to sleep in my house.

"Maybe I could take him bowling," I said to my wife. She was at the draining board doing scalloped potatoes. She put down the knife she was using and turned around.

"If you love me," she said, "you can do this for me. If you don't love me, okay. But if you had a friend, any friend, and the friend came to visit, I'd make him feel comfortable." She wiped her hands with the dish towel.

"I don't have any blind friends," I said.

"You don't have *any* friends," she said. "Period. Besides," she said, "goddamn it, his wife's just died! Don't you understand that? The man's lost his wife!"

I didn't answer. She'd told me a little about the blind man's wife. Her name was Beulah. Beulah! That's a name for a colored woman.

"Was his wife a Negro?" I asked.

"Are you crazy?" my wife said. "Have you just flipped or something?" She picked up a potato. I saw it hit the floor, then roll under the stove. "What's wrong with you?" she said. "Are you drunk?"

"I'm just asking," I said.

Right then my wife filled me in with more detail than I cared to know. I made a drink and sat at the kitchen table to listen. Pieces of the story began to fall into place.

Beulah had gone to work for the blind man the summer after my wife had stopped working for him. Pretty soon Beulah and the blind man had themselves a church wedding. It was a little wedding – who'd want to go to such a wedding in the first place? – just the two of them, plus the minister and the minister's wife. But it was a church wedding just the same. It was what Beulah had wanted, he'd said. But even then Beulah must have been carrying the cancer in her glands. After they had been inseparable for eight years – my wife's word, *inseparable* – Beulah's health went into a rapid decline. She died in a Seattle hospital room, the blind man sitting beside the bed and holding on to her hand. They'd married, lived and worked together, slept together – had sex, sure – and then the blind man had to bury her. All this without his having ever seen what the goddamned woman looked like. It was beyond my understanding. Hearing this, I felt sorry for the blind man for a little bit. And then I found myself thinking what a pitiful life this woman must have led. Imagine a woman who could never see herself as she was seen in the eyes of her loved one. A woman who could go on day after day and never receive the smallest compliment from her beloved. A woman whose husband could never read the expression on her face, be it misery or something better. Someone who could wear makeup or not – what difference to him? She could, if she wanted, wear green eye-shadow around one eye, a straight pin in her nostril, yellow slacks and purple shoes, no matter. And then to slip off into death, the blind man's hand on her hand, his blind eyes streaming tears – I'm imagining now – her last thought maybe this: that he never even knew what she looked like, and she on an express to the grave. Robert was left with a small insurance policy and half of a twenty-peso Mexican coin. The other half of the coin went into the box with her. Pathetic.

So when the time rolled around, my wife went to the depot to pick him up. With nothing to do but wait – sure, I blamed him for that – I was having a drink and watching the TV when I heard the car pull into the drive. I got up from the sofa with my drink and went to the window to have a look.

I saw my wife laughing as she parked the car. I saw her get out of the car and shut the door. She was still wearing a smile. Just amazing. She went around to the other side of the car to where the blind man was already starting to get out. This blind man, feature this, he was wearing a full beard! A beard on a blind man! Too much, I say. The blind man reached into the back seat and dragged out a suitcase. My wife took his arm, shut the car door, and, talking all the way, moved him down the drive and then up the steps to the front porch. I turned off the TV. I finished my drink, rinsed the glass, dried my hands. Then I went to the door.

My wife said, "I want you to meet Robert. Robert, this is my husband. I've told you all about him." She was beaming. She had this blind man by his coat sleeve.

The blind man let go of his suitcase and up came his hand.

I took it. He squeezed hard, held my hand, and then he let it go.

"I feel like we've already met," he boomed.

"Likewise," I said. I didn't know what else to say. Then I said, "Welcome. I've heard a lot about you." We began to move then, a little group, from the porch into the living room, my wife guiding him by the arm. The blind man was carrying his suitcase in his other hand. My wife said things like, "To your left here, Robert. That's right. Now watch it, there's a chair. That's it. Sit down right here. This is the sofa. We just bought this sofa two weeks ago."

I started to say something about the old sofa. I'd liked that old sofa. But I didn't say anything. Then I wanted to say something else, small-talk, about the scenic ride along the Hudson. How going to New York, you should sit on the righthand side of the train, and coming from New York, the lefthand side.

"Did you have a good train ride?" I said. "Which side of the train did you sit on, by the way?"

"What a question, which side!" my wife said. "What's it matter which side?" she said.

"I just asked," I said.

"Right side," the blind man said. "I hadn't been on a train in nearly forty years. Not since I was a kid. With my folks. That's been a long time. I'd nearly forgotten the sensation. I have winter in my beard now," he said. "So I've been told, anyway. Do I look distinguished, my dear?" the blind man said to my wife.

"You look distinguished, Robert," she said. "Robert," she said. "Robert, it's just so good to see you."

My wife finally took her eyes off the blind man and looked at me. I had the feeling she didn't like what she saw. I shrugged.

I've never met, or personally known, anyone who was blind. This blind man was late forties, a heavy-set, balding man with stooped shoulders, as if he carried a great weight there. He wore brown slacks, brown shoes, a light-brown shirt, a tie, a sports coat. Spiffy. He also had this full beard. But he didn't use a cane and he didn't wear dark glasses. I'd always thought dark glasses were a must for the blind. Fact was, I wished he had a pair. At first glance, his eyes looked like anyone else's eyes. But if you looked close, there was something different about them. Too much white in the iris, for one thing, and the pupils seemed to move around in the sockets without his knowing it or being able to stop it. Creepy. As I stared at his face, I saw the left pupil turn in toward his nose while the other made an effort to keep in one place. But it was only an effort, for that eye was on the roam without his knowing it or wanting it to be.

I said, "Let me get you a drink. What's your pleasure? We have a little of everything. It's one of our pastimes."

"Bub, I'm a Scotch man myself," he said fast enough in this big voice.

"Right," I said. Bub! "Sure you are. I knew it."

He let his fingers touch his suitcase, which was sitting alongside the sofa. He was taking his bearings. I didn't blame him for that.

"I'll move that up to your room," my wife said.

"No, that's fine," the blind man said loudly. "It can go up when I go up."

"A little water with the Scotch?" I said.

"Very little" he said.

"I knew it," I said.

He said, "Just a tad. The Irish actor, Barry Fitzgerald? I'm like that fellow. When I drink water, Fitzgerald said, I drink water. When I drink whiskey, I drink whiskey." My wife laughed. The blind man brought his hand up under his beard. He lifted his beard slowly and let it drop.

I did the drinks, three big glasses of Scotch with a splash of water in each. Then we made ourselves comfortable and talked about Robert's travels. First the long flight from the West Coast to Connecticut, we covered that. Then from Connecticut up here by train. We had another drink concerning that leg of the trip.

I remembered having read somewhere that the blind didn't smoke because, as speculation had it, they couldn't see the smoke they exhaled. I thought I knew that much and that much only about blind people. But this blind man smoked his cigarette down to the nubbin and then lit another one. This blind man filled his ashtray and my wife emptied it.

When we sat down at the table for dinner, we had another drink. My wife heaped Robert's plate with cube

steak, scalloped potatoes, green beans. I buttered him up two
slices of bread. I said, "Here's bread and butter for you."
I swallowed some of my drink. "Now let us pray," I said, and
the blind man lowered his head. My wife looked at me, her
mouth agape. "Pray the phone won't ring and the food
doesn't get cold," I said.

We dug in. We ate everything there was to eat on the table.
We ate like there was no tomorrow. We didn't talk. We ate.
We scarfed. We grazed that table. We were into serious eating.
The blind man had right away located his foods, he knew
just where everything was on his plate. I watched with
admiration as he used his knife and fork on the meat. He'd
cut two pieces of meat, fork the meat into his mouth, and
then go all out for the scalloped potatoes, the beans next,
and then he'd tear off a hunk of buttered bread and eat that.
He'd follow this up with a big drink of milk. It didn't seem
to bother him to use his fingers once in a while, either.

We finished everything, including half a strawberry pie.

For a few moments, we sat as if stunned. Sweat beaded on
our faces. Finally, we got up from the table and left the dirty
plates. We didn't look back. We took ourselves into the living
room and sank into our places again. Robert and my wife
sat on the sofa. I took the big chair. We had us two or three
more drinks while they talked about the major things that
had come to pass for them in the past ten years. For the most
part, I just listened. Now and then I joined in. I didn't want
him to think I'd left the room, and I didn't want her to think
I was feeling left out. They talked of things that had
happened to them – to them! – these past ten years. I waited
in vain to hear my name on my wife's sweet lips: "And then
my dear husband came into my life" – something like that.
But I heard nothing of the sort. More talk of Robert. Robert
had done a little of everything, it seemed, a regular blind

jack-of-all-trades. But most recently he and his wife had had an Amway distributorship, from which, I gathered, they'd earned their living, such as it was. The blind man was also a ham radio operator. He talked in his loud voice about conversations he'd had with fellow operators in Guam, in the Philippines, in Alaska, and even in Tahiti. He said he'd have a lot of friends there if he ever wanted to go visit those places. From time to time, he'd turn his blind face toward me, put his hand under his beard, ask me something. How long had I been in my present position? (Three years.) Did I like my work? (I didn't.) Was I going to stay with it? (What were the options?) Finally, when I thought he was beginning to run down, I got up and turned on the TV.

My wife looked at me with irritation. She was heading toward a boil. Then she looked at the blind man and said, "Robert, do you have a TV?"

The blind man said, "My dear, I have two TVs. I have a color set and a black-and-white thing, an old relic. It's funny, but if I turn the TV on, and I'm always turning it on, I turn on the color set. It's funny, don't you think?"

I didn't know what to say to that. I had absolutely nothing to say to that. No opinion. So I watched the news program and tried to listen to what the announcer was saying.

"This is a color TV," the blind man said. "Don't ask me how, but I can tell."

"We traded up a while ago," I said.

The blind man had another taste of his drink. He lifted his beard, sniffed it, and let it fall. He leaned forward on the sofa. He positioned his ashtray on the coffee table, then put the lighter to his cigarette. He leaned back on the sofa and crossed his legs at the ankles.

My wife covered her mouth, and then she yawned. She stretched. She said, "I think I'll go upstairs and put on my robe. I think I'll change into something else. Robert, you make yourself comfortable," she said.

"I'm comfortable," the blind man said.

"I want you to feel comfortable in this house," she said.

"I am comfortable," the blind man said.

After she'd left the room, he and I listened to the weather report and then to the sports roundup. By that time, she'd been gone so long I didn't know if she was going to come back. I thought she might have gone to bed. I wished she'd come back downstairs. I didn't want to be left alone with a blind man. I asked him if he wanted another drink, and he said sure. Then I asked if he wanted to smoke some dope with me. I said I'd just rolled a number. I hadn't, but I planned to do so in about two shakes.

"I'll try some with you," he said.

"Damn right," I said. "That's the stuff."

I got our drinks and sat down on the sofa with him. Then I rolled us two fat numbers. I lit one and passed it. I brought it to his fingers. He took it and inhaled.

"Hold it as long as you can," I said. I could tell he didn't know the first thing.

My wife came back downstairs wearing her pink robe and her pink slippers.

"What do I smell?" she said.

"We thought we'd have us some cannabis," I said.

My wife gave me a savage look. Then she looked at the blind man and said, "Robert, I didn't know you smoked."

He said, "I do now, my dear. There's a first time for everything. But I don't feel anything yet."

"This stuff is pretty mellow," I said. "This stuff is mild. It's dope you can reason with," I said. "It doesn't mess you up.

"Not much it doesn't, bub," he said, and laughed.

My wife sat on the sofa between the blind man and me. I passed her the number. She took it and toked and then passed it back to me. "Which way is this going?" she said. Then she said, "I shouldn't be smoking this. I can hardly keep my eyes open as it is. That dinner did me in. I shouldn't have eaten so much."

"It was the strawberry pie," the blind man said. "That's what did it," he said, and he laughed his big laugh. Then he shook his head.

"There's more strawberry pie," I said.

"Do you want some more, Robert?" my wife said.

"Maybe in a little while," he said.

We gave our attention to the TV. My wife yawned again. She said, "Your bed is made up when you feel like going to bed, Robert. I know you must have had a long day. When you're ready to go to bed, say so." She pulled his arm. "Robert?"

He came to and said, "I've had a real nice time. This beats tapes, doesn't it?"

I said, "Coming at you," and I put the number between his fingers. He inhaled, held the smoke, and then let it go. It was like he'd been doing it since he was nine years old.

"Thanks, bub," he said. "But I think this is all for me. I think I'm beginning to feel it," he said. He held the burning roach out for my wife.

"Same here," she said. "Ditto. Me, too." She took the roach and passed it to me. "I may just sit here for a while between you two guys with my eyes closed. But don't let me bother you, okay? Either one of you. If it bothers you, say so. Otherwise, I may just sit here with my eyes closed until you're ready to go to bed," she said. "Your bed's made up, Robert, when you're ready. It's right next to our room at the top of the stairs. We'll show you up when you're ready. You wake me up now, you guys, if I fall asleep." She said that and then she closed her eyes and went to sleep.

The news program ended. I got up and changed the channel. I sat back down on the sofa. I wished my wife hadn't pooped out. Her head lay across the back of the sofa, her mouth open. She'd turned so that her robe had slipped away from her legs, exposing a juicy thigh. I reached to draw her robe back over her, and it was then that I glanced at the blind man. What the hell! I flipped the robe open again.

"You say when you want some strawberry pie," I said.

"I will," he said.

I said, "Are you tired? Do you want me to take you up to your bed? Are you ready to hit the hay?"

"Not yet," he said. "No, I'll stay up with you, bub. If that's all right. I'll stay up until you're ready to turn in. We haven't had a chance to talk. Know what I mean? I feel like me and her monopolized the evening." He lifted his beard and he let it fall. He picked up his cigarettes and his lighter.

"That's all right," I said. Then I said, "I'm glad for the company."

And I guess I was. Every night I smoked dope and stayed up as long as I could before I fell asleep. My wife and I hardly ever went to bed at the same time. When I did go to sleep, I had these dreams. Sometimes I'd wake up from one of them, my heart going crazy.

Something about the church and the Middle Ages was on the TV. Not your run-of-the-mill TV fare. I wanted to watch something else. I turned to the other channels. But there was nothing on them, either. So I turned back to the first channel and apologized.

"Bub, it's all right," the blind man said. "It's fine with me. Whatever you want to watch is okay. I'm always learning something. Learning never ends. It won't hurt me to learn something tonight. I got ears," he said.

We didn't say anything for a time. He was leaning forward with his head turned at me, his right ear aimed in the direction of the set. Very disconcerting. Now and then his eyelids drooped and then they snapped open again. Now and then he put his fingers into his beard and tugged, like he was thinking about something he was hearing on the television.

On the screen, a group of men wearing cowls was being set upon and tormented by men dressed in skeleton costumes and men dressed as devils. The men dressed as devils wore devil masks, horns, and long tails. This pageant was part of a procession. The Englishman who was narrating the thing said it took place in Spain once a year. I tried to explain to the blind man what was happening.

"Skeletons," he said. "I know about skeletons," he said, and he nodded.

The TV showed this one cathedral. Then there was a long, slow look at another one. Finally, the picture switched to the famous one in Paris, with its flying buttresses and its spires reaching up to the clouds. The camera pulled away to show the whole of the cathedral rising above the skyline.

There were times when the Englishman who was telling the thing would shut up, would simply let the camera move around over the cathedrals. Or else the camera would tour the countryside, men in fields walking behind oxen. I waited as long as I could. Then I felt I had to say something. I said, "They're showing the outside of this cathedral now. Gargoyles. Little statues carved to look like monsters. Now I guess they're in Italy. Yeah, they're in Italy. There's paintings on the walls of this one church."

"Are those fresco paintings, bub?" he asked, and he sipped from his drink.

I reached for my glass. But it was empty. I tried to remember what I could remember. "You're asking me are those frescoes?" I said. "That's a good question. I don't know."

The camera moved to a cathedral outside Lisbon. The differences in the Portuguese cathedral compared with the French and Italian were not that great. But they were there. Mostly the interior stuff. Then something occurred to me, and I said, "Something has occurred to me. Do you have any idea what a cathedral is? What they look like, that is? Do you follow me? If somebody says cathedral to you, do you have any notion what they're talking about? Do you know the difference between that and a Baptist church, say?"

He let the smoke dribble from his mouth. "I know they took hundreds of workers fifty or a hundred years to build," he said. "I just heard the man say that, of course. I know generations of the same families worked on a cathedral. I heard him say that, too. The men who began their life's work on them, they never lived to see the completion of their work. In that wise, bub, they're no different from the rest of us, right?" He laughed. Then his eyelids drooped again. His head nodded. He seemed to be snoozing. Maybe he was imagining himself in Portugal. The TV was showing another cathedral now. This one was in Germany. The Englishman's voice droned on. "Cathedrals," the blind man said. He sat up and rolled his head back and forth. "If you want the truth, bub, that's about all I know. What I just said. What I heard him say. But maybe you could describe one to me? I wish you'd do it. I'd like that. If you want to know, I really don't have a good idea."

I stared hard at the shot of the cathedral on the TV. How

could I even begin to describe it? But say my life depended on it. Say my life was being threatened by an insane guy who said I had to do it or else.

I stared some more at the cathedral before the picture flipped off into the countryside. There was no use. I turned to the blind man and said, "To begin with, they're very tall." I was looking around the room for clues. "They reach way up. Up and up. Toward the sky. They're so big, some of them, they have to have these supports. To help hold them up, so to speak. These supports are called buttresses. They remind me of viaducts, for some reason. But maybe you don't know viaducts, either? Sometimes the cathedrals have devils and such carved into the front. Sometimes lords and ladies. Don't ask me why this is," I said.

He was nodding. The whole upper part of his body seemed to be moving back and forth.

"I'm not doing so good, am I?" I said.

He stopped nodding and leaned forward on the edge of the sofa. As he listened to me, he was running his fingers through his beard. I wasn't getting through to him, I could see that. But he waited for me to go on just the same. He nodded, like he was trying to encourage me. I tried to think what else to say. "They're really big," I said. "They're massive. They're built of stone. Marble, too, sometimes. In those olden days, when they built cathedrals, men wanted to be close to God. In those olden days, God was an important part of everyone's life. You could tell this from their cathedral-building. I'm sorry," I said, "but it looks like that's the best I can do for you. I'm just no good at it."

"That's all right, bub," the blind man said. "Hey, listen. I hope you don't mind my asking you. Can I ask you some-thing? Let me ask you a simple question, yes or no. I'm just curious and there's no offense. You're my host. But let me ask if you are in any way religious? You don't mind my asking?"

I shook my head. He couldn't see that, though. A wink is the same as a nod to a blind man. "I guess I don't believe in it. In anything. Sometimes it's hard. You know what I'm saying?"

"Sure, I do," he said.

"Right," I said.

The Englishman was still holding forth. My wife sighed in her sleep. She drew a long breath and went on with her sleeping.

"You'll have to forgive me," I said. "But I can't tell you what a cathedral looks like. It just isn't in me to do it. I can't do any more than I've done."

The blind man sat very still, his head down, as he listened to me.

I said, "The truth is, cathedrals don't mean anything special to me. Nothing. Cathedrals. They're something to look at on late-night TV. That's all they are."

It was then that the blind man cleared his throat. He brought something up. He took a handkerchief from his back pocket. Then he said, "I get it, bub. It's okay. It happens. Don't worry about it," he said. "Hey, listen to me. Will you do me a favor? I got an idea. Why don't you find us some heavy paper? And a pen. We'll do something. We'll draw one together. Get us a pen and some heavy paper. Go on, bub, get the stuff," he said.

So I went upstairs. My legs felt like they didn't have any strength in them. They felt like they did after I'd done some running. In my wife's room, I looked around. I found some ballpoints in a little basket on her table. And then I tried to think where to look for the kind of paper he was talking about.

Downstairs, in the kitchen, I found a shopping bag with

onion skins in the bottom of the bag. I emptied the bag and shook it. I brought it into the living room and sat down with it near his legs. I moved some things, smoothed the wrinkles from the bag, spread it out on the coffee table.

The blind man got down from the sofa and sat next to me on the carpet.

He ran his fingers over the paper. He went up and down the sides of the paper. The edges, even the edges. He fingered the corners.

"All right," he said. "All right, let's do her."

He found my hand, the hand with the pen. He closed his hand over my hand. "Go ahead, bub, draw," he said. "Draw. You'll see. I'll follow along with you. It'll be okay. Just begin now like I'm telling you. You'll see. Draw," the blind man said.

So I began. First I drew a box that looked like a house. It could have been the house I lived in. Then I put a roof on it. At either end of the roof, I drew spires. Crazy.

"Swell," he said. "Terrific. You're doing fine," he said. "Never thought anything like this could happen in your life-time, did you, bub? Well, it's a strange life, we all know that. Go on now. Keep it up."

I put in windows with arches. I drew flying buttresses. I hung great doors. I couldn't stop. The TV station went off the air. I put down the pen and closed and opened my fingers. The blind man felt around over the paper. He moved the tips of his fingers over the paper, all over what I had drawn, and he nodded.

"Doing fine," the blind man said.

I took up the pen again, and he found my hand. I kept at it. I'm no artist. But I kept drawing just the same.

My wife opened up her eyes and gazed at us. She sat up on the sofa, her robe hanging open. She said, "What are you doing? Tell me, I want to know."

I didn't answer her.

The blind man said, "We're drawing a cathedral. Me and him are working on it. Press hard," he said to me. "That's right. That's good," he said. "Sure. You got it, bub. I can tell. You didn't think you could. But you can, can't you? You're cooking with gas now. You know what I'm saying? We're going to really have us something here in a minute. How's the old arm?" he said "Put some people in there now. What's a cathedral without people?"

My wife said, "What's going on? Robert, what are you doing? What's going on?"

"It's all right," he said to her. "Close your eyes now," the blind man said to me.

I did it. I closed them just like he said.

"Are they closed?" he said. "Don't fudge."

"They're closed," I said.

"Keep them that way," he said. He said, "Don't stop now. Draw."

So we kept on with it. His fingers rode my fingers as my hand went over the paper. It was like nothing else in my life up to now.

Then he said, "I think that's it. I think you got it," he said. "Take a look. What do you think?"

But I had my eyes closed. I thought I'd keep them that way for a little longer. I thought it was something I ought to do.

"Well?" he said. "Are you looking?"

My eyes were still closed. I was in my house. I knew that. But I didn't feel like I was inside anything.

"It's really something," I said.